Jack O' Knaves

Jack's adventures continue as he becomes both outlaw and lover

ROBERT ASTON

The Knave of Hearts, he stole some tarts

Pen Press

© Robert Aston 2014

All rights reserved

No part of this publication may be reproduced, stored in a retrieval system, or transmitted in any form or by any means, without the prior permission in writing of the publisher, nor be otherwise circulated in any form of binding or cover other than that in which it is published and without a similar condition including this condition being imposed on the subsequent purchaser.

First published in Great Britain by Pen Press

All paper used in the printing of this book has been made from wood grown in managed, sustainable forests.

ISBN13: 978-1-78003-484-3

Printed and bound in the UK
Pen Press is an imprint of
Indepenpress Publishing Limited
25 Eastern Place
Brighton
BN2 1GJ

A catalogue record of this book is available from
The British Library

Cover design by Jacqueline Abromeit

Acknowledgements

As was the case with *Jack o' Beans*, I am greatly indebted to Robert Taylor of *The Black Country Bugle* for editing the series of stories that form the greater part of this work.

Thanks also to those persons who provided information around which this story is based. To mention but a few, John Hemingway and Adrian Durkin for their excellent works of reference; and Alan Harvey for his artefacts.

A special thank you to the staff at Coseley Library for obtaining reference works from Dudley and beyond.

Heartfelt gratitude to my wife Janet for her continued tolerance and encouragement.

And of course, to the staff at Indepenpress for transforming these words into a book that is suitable for presenting to you, the public.

Robert Aston

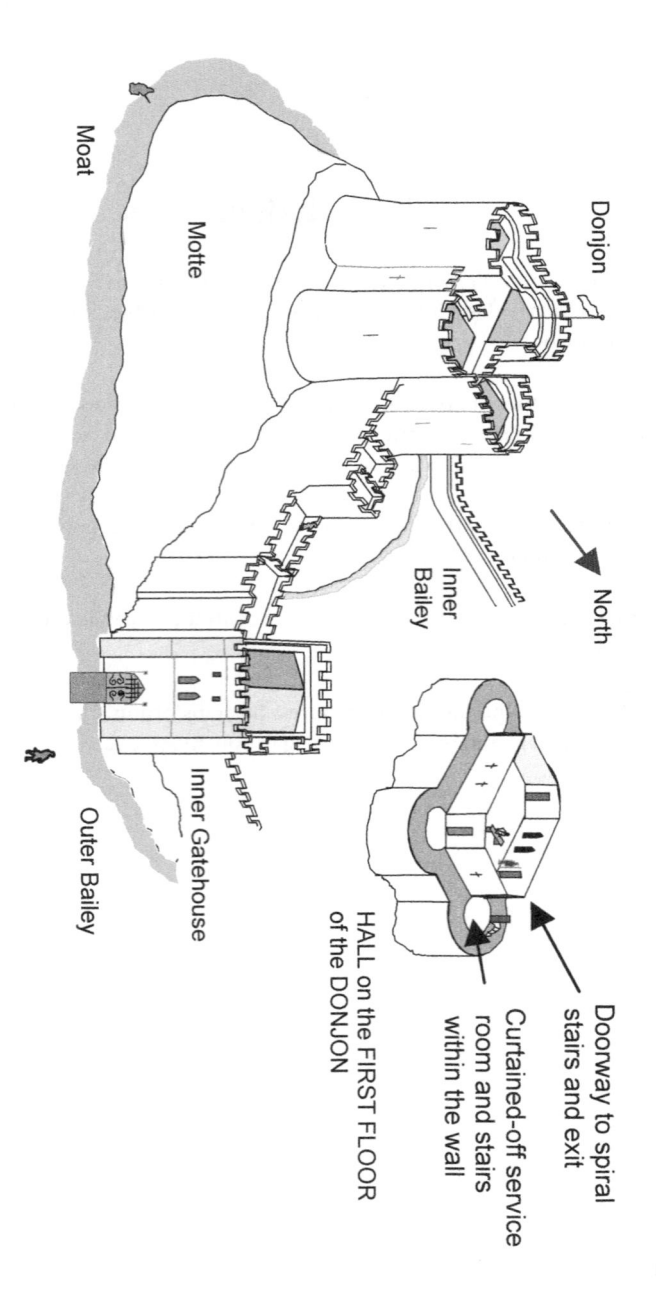

Dudley Castle Donjon and Inner Gatehouse

Donjon

Motte

Moat

Inner Bailey

North

Inner Gatehouse

Outer Bailey

Doorway to spiral stairs and exit

Curtained-off service room and stairs within the wall

HALL on the FIRST FLOOR of the DONJON

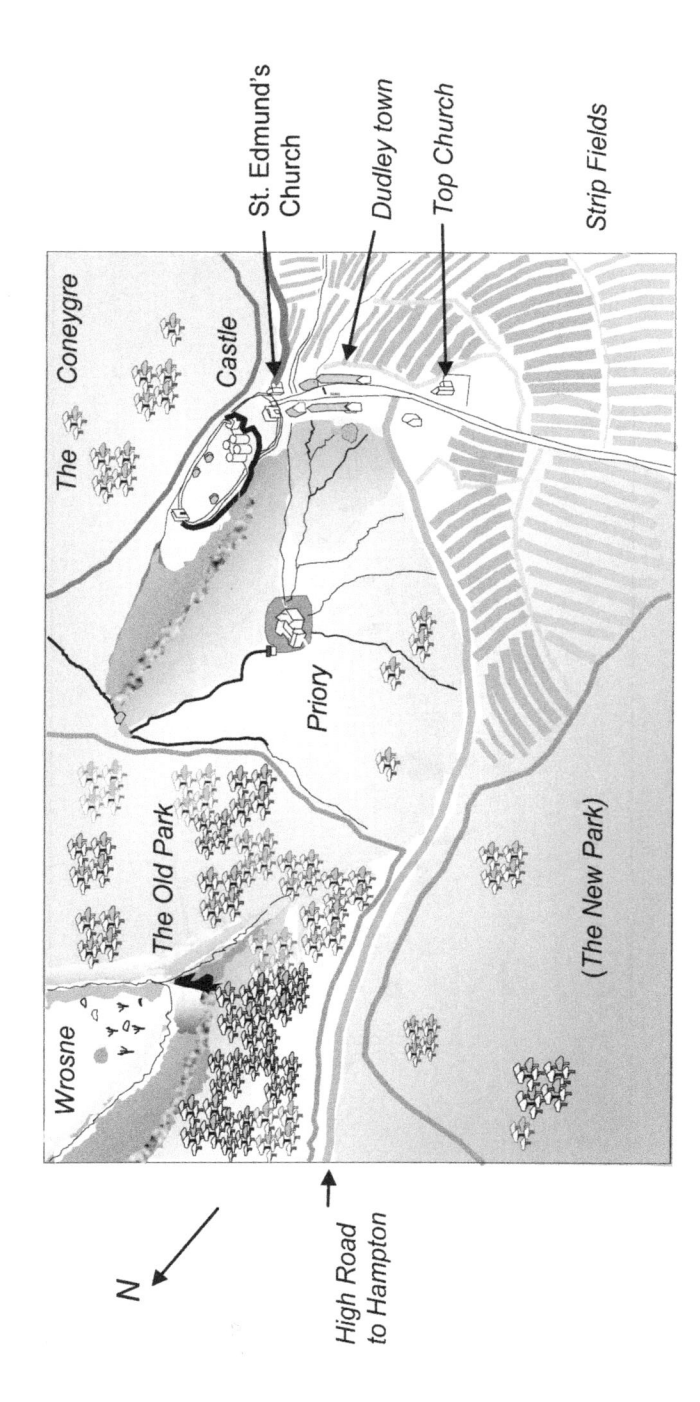

The Lie of the Land

Dudley Priory, *circa* **1315**
(an idealised reconstruction)

Lych Gate

N

Glossary

Aketon: Padded garment, worn to protect the torso.
Ar, Arr, Arrr: Yes (with varying length and intensity).
Arrow-loop, Loophole: Opening for shooting arrows through.
Baxter: Female baker.
Bodkin: Sharply-pointed arrowhead.
Bolt: Short arrow, used with a crossbow.
Canstow?: Can you?
Cookney: Assistant to a cook.
Coney: Adult rabbit.
Crenels: Spaces on battlements for the use of bows.
Crustades: Pastries.
Diaper: Piece of fabric.
Embrasure: Bevelled sides of a window or door opening.
Fletchings: Feathers or flights of an arrow.
Ganache: Poncho-like garment with wide sleeves.
Greaves: Shin guards. Usually of leather or metal.
Groat: Four pence silver piece
Hauberk: Shirt of maile.
Lancet: Tall, narrow wind-eye, usually pointed at the top.
Lant-horn: Lantern.
Liripipe: Tubular extension at the back of a hood.
Longshanks: Nickname of King Edward (later called 'the First').
Maile: Interlocking rings of iron. Used for armour.
Nobs: Short for nobles.
Nock: Hard pieces at the ends of a bow, grooved to take the string.
Pavise: Man-sized shield designed to stand upright on the ground.
Pile: Business end of an arrow or bolt.
Poleyn: Protective armour for the kneecap. Usually of steel or leather.
Rovers: An archery contest that's played over open ground.
Saddleback: Ridge that is higher at both ends.
Sooth: Truth.
Tump: Tumulus. Prehistoric grave mound.
Undrentide: Midday.
Wazzin: Gullet. Throat.
Willtow?: Shortened form of 'Wilt thou?' (Will you?)
Whum: Home.
Wind-eye: Window
Yow, Yoh: You (pronunciation dating from Saxon times.)

Foreword

Thirteen years have elapsed since Jack and his gran were first set to work in the bakehouse of Dudley Castle. But to his grandmother's dismay and annoyance, Jack had become bored with his life as a cookney and enrolled as a trainee soldier.

"You will get yourself killed," she'd wailed, having managed to teach her mouth to say 'you' instead of 'yow' at last.

"No I won't," he'd hastened to reassure her. "Everything's quiet and peaceful up here. I shan't have to do any actual fighting."

How wrong he was.

England is in turmoil.

King 'Longshanks' has died without managing to subdue the Scots.

His son – the second Edward in the Plantagenet line – has been beaten back by the Scots at Bannockburn. And if that wasn't enough of a set-back, by bestowing great wealth on his favourites, the king has aroused the enmity of the Earl of Lancaster – his most powerful baron.

John de Somery of Dudley remains staunchly loyal to the crown – having sworn fealty before God when knighted by both monarchs. But at *what* cost to himself… and his young retainer?

Part One

Jack in the Stocks

CHAPTER 1

"Canstow spare some o' yer grandmother's crustades, Cousin Jacob?"

The soldier's mouth, just visible beneath his visor, lost its cheerful smirk. As the guard at the Outer Gatehouse of Dudley Castle, he'd been contemplating the matchless charms of the Steward's daughter. Thrusting up the visor, he peered down at the urchin who was gazing beseechingly up at him. The boy's clothes hung loosely on his slender frame. Although heavily patched and mended, they looked surprisingly clean. After making sure that no one else could hear, the guard squared his shoulders and puffed out his chest.

"Clear off," he hissed, as loudly as he dared.

"You'm Cousin Jacob, bain't yer?" Rivulets of tears ran down the boy's cheeks and a dew-drop glistened on the end of his nose. "Mother says as I be related to yow."

The guard paused. Jacob was the name that he'd been christened with. However, after a brief spell of calling himself Jacques, he was now known by everyone as Jack. Hearing his old name uttered at the town gate was an unwelcome reminder of his humble beginnings. When he was a boy, his grandmother had been abducted from her cottage in Netherton to bake pastries for the Baron. Jack had been brought along to assist her, but continued to dream of becoming a soldier and wearing splendid armour. So now that he was old enough, he'd enrolled as a trainee guard. Gran resented this at first, but had become resigned to it at last. "After all," she'd admitted, "the higher in the ranks you rise, the safer our family will be." And apparently, one of that family was standing in front of him now.

"What is thy name?" Jack asked in as commanding a voice as he could manage.

"Isaiah," replied the boy, wiping his nose on his sleeve. "But everybody calls me Zarn." He pressed his hands together in a gesture of prayer. "Please help us, Cousin Jacob. We've had hardly anythin' to eat at home for four days now."

'Home' meant the nearby village of Netherton. Jack's family had lived there for generations – from a time before the Normans came to make servants of them all. But this was not the place or the time to enquire further.

"Wait over there, wiltow?" Jack nodded towards a group of washerwomen who were scrubbing and gossiping at the nearby spring. Because the water bubbled up on the ridge between the castle and the town, it was said to be the spot where Saint Edmund jabbed his staff into the ground. Further irritated by that silly superstition, Jack jabbed the iron-shod heel of his spear down hard on the cobbled forecourt. Hearing the impact, his fellow guard peered over the battlements of the gatehouse.

"Art thow all right, Jack?" the guard called down anxiously.

"Fine," Jack answered, raising his visor again – this time to show his friend a reassuring grin. Turning, he called out after the boy: "I'll be finished here soon."

And about time too, he thought. A sudden shower had soaked his padded aketon and it steamed and sweated in the heat of the noonday sun. Fortunately, he would soon be relieved of duty and could take the boy up to meet his gran. She'd undoubtedly be pleased to see him, having received little news from home for ages.

As soon as Jack had been replaced at the gate, he beckoned for the boy to follow as he returned his spear to the weapon store. After getting the lad signed in on the record sheet for the day, he marched briskly up the hill, his scabbard marking time as it rapped the leather poleyn on his knee.

Zarn hurried along behind, amazed by the armour of the soldiers that they passed. Although the men greeted his cousin Jacob as a friend, they completely ignored the labourers who toiled and sweated at the roadside.

On reaching the top of the incline, a scene of heroic splendour met their eyes. Archers were sending arrows swooping across the butts. Paired warriors hacked enthusiastically at one another's shields. Colourfully-dressed ladies were strolling about and fluttering their eyelashes at the men. And above all this activity, the drum towers of the donjon rose in gleaming white splendour against the clear blue sky.

Jack's first sight of the outer bailey had been very different. But most of the building work was finished now, and the lime kilns were no longer spewing their evil-smelling fumes over the ground. Jack breathed in deeply, enjoying the sweet scents of roses and thyme.

Scuttling along at Jack's side, Zarn stared around in wonder. Everybody looked so well fed. For as long as he could remember, he'd been hungry. On the long winter evenings, his mother would huddle him close to the fire in the middle of their cottage and tell him about the good old days. Food had been plentiful then, and even the beggars could find enough to eat. But the weather had turned colder and wetter, and the crops had failed year upon year. Their pig had been slaughtered long since – his mother hoarding the last precious scraps of bacon rind until they too had been eaten. With her latest babby dying in her arms, she had swallowed her pride and sent Zarn to beg a few scraps from her kinfolk at the castle – relatives that he'd heard about but never met.

By now, the ill-matched pair had left the outer bailey and were clattering across a drawbridge to present themselves at the inner gatehouse. Above their heads, iron-plated fangs hung poised as if ready to bite. Undeterred, Jack drew his sword and thumped its pommel on a great oak door. A trap slid back and a password whispered. Ornate hinges groaned in protest as the door opened enough to allow them through. The door banged shut behind them, enclosing them in a long, dark tunnel whose only source of light was a trapdoor in the barrel-vaulted ceiling. The light grew even dimmer as a bearded face peered down at them.

"What yer got there, Jack? Been sowing yer wild oats in the stews?"

Jack blushed at the implication.

"Nay!" he protested. "This is a relative of mine – come to visit my gran."

"I thought he featured thee," chortled the man.

The light increased as the man's head was withdrawn – and was then extinguished as the trap crashed down. Stumbling along in almost complete darkness, Jack felt trembling fingers clutching at his arm.

"Don't worry," he whispered, unlatching a door in the inner gate. "It's through here."

They stepped out into a courtyard – an acre and a half of trampled earth and fine stone buildings – completely enclosed by high and battlemented walls. The only thing moving was a column of smoke that was rising from a chimney not far away. Jack grinned as he remembered the ramshackle bakehouse that once stood there. This new one was built from limestone blocks, with tiles on the roof instead of thatch.

*

Hearing the patter of tiny feet approaching her threshold, Jack's grandmother turned enquiringly away from her pastry table.

"Why Jacob, who is this little 'un that you've brought to see me?"

"He says that he's a relative of ours," Jack replied. "His real name is Isaiah, although he likes to be called Zarn."

"Oh, you *men*," Gran said, smiling broadly. "Never satisfied with the good Christian names that we choose for yer." She wiped her floured hands on her clean white apron. "Look at me, Isaiah. There's nothing to be afraid of here. Now tell me: who is thy mother?"

"Ruth," replied the boy, still staring self-consciously at his feet.

"Ah, *now* I know who you are," Gran exclaimed, rushing forward to land a bristly kiss on his cheek. "Yow was only a babby when last I seed thee." She'd reverted to their old way of speaking to put the boy at his ease. "Now tell me all the news. For a start: have yer any brothers or sisters?"

"Ar, missus. I have a little brother an' sister back whum."

"And what are their names?"

Zarn told her.

"And how are thy parents, boy?"

"Not good, missus," Zarn said sorrowfully. "Mom has no meat to feed us. Dad went off lookin' for work but it looks as if 'e ain't a-comin' back. Mom says that unless there's a miracle, none of us am goin' to make it through to the harvest."

"Why didn't she come up and ask me herself?"

"She thinks that you won't want to know her now that you'm livin' up 'ere with the nobs. She's waitin' for me down at that spring by Saint Edmund's Church."

"Well you can tell 'er that we'll always be glad to see 'er. In the meantime…" She dragged a three-legged stool from beneath the table and set it down close to the oven, whose whitewashed stonework radiated comforting warmth. "Sit yerself down while I see what I've got to tide thee over."

After covering her pastry with a cloth, she began to select some tarts from the tray beside her. "Here," she said, offering one to the boy. "Get this down thy wazzin."

As the boy crammed it into his mouth, she questioned him further about the fortunes of their family. A dozen crustades later, she called across to Jack who was slouching in the doorway. Above his head, a thin wooden shelf sagged beneath piles of empty sacks.

"Get us one of them sacks down wiltow, Jacob," Gran said, pointing.

Irritated by her continual refusal to use his adopted name, Jack drew his sword from its scabbard and hooked down one of the sacks with the hilt.

"Thanks, Gran," he spluttered through billowing clouds of flour dust. "You'll get me put on a charge for this!" With the flour turning to paste on his wet aketon, he tried to scrape it off with the edge of his blade. It only made things worse.

"Never mind that," Gran retorted. "Just bring that sack over here and hold it open."

*

"And where are you going with *that*?"

The latest guard at the castle's Outer Gatehouse had emerged just in time to see Jack waving off a small boy. The boy was pushing a four-wheeled cart. The cart contained a bulging, flour-covered sack.

"It's all right John," Jack shouted, turning round. His face fell. It wasn't his friend after all. It was his bitterest enemy.

CHAPTER 2

"So *this* is how you repay our hospitality!"

The Steward of Dudley Castle shifted awkwardly in his chair, furious at being awakened from his afternoon nap. He peered in turn at each of the three individuals who had been marched up to the Great Hall of the Donjon by the guard who now stood smirking in its doorway. He knew the swordsman and the woman fairly well, although the urchin cowering between them was a stranger.

The man had been but a boy when he'd first appeared in the castle. How could he forget it? He'd had the cheek to try to sell him a bag of mysterious beans. Assuming them to be of little worth, the Steward had tossed them into the brazier– whereupon the fumes had rendered everyone in the hall unconscious.

However, that unfortunate incident *had* allowed him to track down the baxter of the Baron's favourite crustades. She was standing before him now – as thin as a rake and as narrow-eyed and truculent as ever. When she'd been brought to live in the castle, Jack o' Beans (as the man was then laughingly known) had been allowed to come as her helper. Rebellious from the start, he'd been selected to be the arrow-boy for the day of that fateful deer hunt.

Although there were many witnesses to Lord Roger's murder, the boy had been the only member of the party who could identify the killer. So the Baron had used him as bait to lure the murderer out. But when that man attacked, the boy had hacked him to death with Will Hawkes's broken sword. Now fully grown, he'd been training as a foot soldier. The Steward had to admit that he *did* look the part: now almost six feet tall and correspondingly broad of shoulder.

Suddenly aware of the scrutiny, the young man stood stiffly to attention, his left hand resting lightly on the pommel of his sword – his right arm cradling his helmet like a sleeping baby.

Clearly visible in the light from the lancet wind-eyes, incriminating traces of flour besmeared his padded aketon.

"I thought better of thee than *this*," the Steward barked as he picked up a sheet of parchment and held it near to a candle.

The hall fell silent, except for crackling of flames in the brazier and a rumbling from the hound that lay basking in its warmth. Tattered war-banners hung down from the raftered ceiling, swaying in the updraught from the fire. Jack had been cherishing hopes of achieving glory in the service of those flags, but now his gran had scuppered that with her reckless foolishness.

"It says here that you are getting quite proficient with the bow," the Steward murmured thoughtfully, "and with that sword of yours – or rather: *ours*!"

At a signal to the guard, Jack's hand was swept unceremoniously from the pommel of his sword. To the sighing of steel against leather, the weapon was slid from its sheath. This was terrible. Jack had devoted himself to the task of mastering that weapon – urged on by the man whose life he'd once saved. He still thought of Will Hawkes as *the* Forester, although he was only one of several who controlled the hunting parks.

"And it also says that you swing a battleaxe with ease and purpose."

Jack's expression had grown even more sullen and shamefaced. He'd noticed a movement of the curtain at the far end of the hall. Could the Steward's daughter be concealed behind it? Would she (shame of all shame) witness his disgrace?

"And it seems that your training has not been without blemish," continued the Steward curtly. "Apparently, you crippled a fellow recruit. He still cannot walk, by the way!" Tossing the document aside, he stood up. Leaning forward, and with both fists on the table, he stared Jack in the eyes.

"Since you have been caught stealing," he said menacingly, "I am required by law to hand you over to the Sheriff of Staffordshire."

Before Jack could absorb the full importance of these words, the curtain was flung back and a young woman dashed across the floor to the Steward's side. Her face was flushed, almost as red as the dress that she clutched to her bosom – a bosom that Jack had admired when she'd appeared in the courtyard below. On that horrible occasion of the accident, he'd been trying to impress her with his prowess as a swordsman.

"He is but a poor lad," the girl wailed, hanging on her father's arm, "so he won't be able to bribe the sheriff. He could have his hands chopped off."

"He should have thought of that before he stole those crustades."

"THEM CRUSTADES WAS ALL STALE," Gran cried, rushing to the table, "and they'm not even fit for pigs."

For a moment, the Steward thought that she was referring to himself and his men. However, her anxious expression suggested that this was probably not the case.

There was a commotion at the door that led out onto the spiral staircase. The Chef emerged, breathless and enraged. "You lie, you old crow!" he cried, hurrying forward to confront her. "I have tasted those pies for myself, and I cannot detect any fault in them."

Jack's grandmother thrust out her chin in defiance. "Why does that not surprise me?" she screeched. "Considering the tasteless rubbish that yow serve up." In her anxiety she'd unconsciously lapsed into her erstwhile way of speaking.

As the Chef swelled up with anger and indignation, the old woman turned back to the Steward – just in time to see the corners of his mouth twitch as he hastily suppressed a grin. Inferring that he shared her opinion, she opened her mouth to press home her advantage. Then she shut it again. It was never wise to upset those who'd been put in charge of you; they always found a way of getting back at you. Nevertheless, her confidence had received a much-needed boost.

"I do *not* lie, my lord," she protested. "Those crusts were not fit for the gentry. Nor for the soldiers. Nor for anyone else in the castle." Hitching up her hessian skirts, she rested clenched fists on her scrawny hips. "I could see no 'arm in sending some leftovers to my poor starving relatives down there." She nodded towards the nearest arrow-loop wind-eye, where the tower of Top Church could be seen on the distant skyline. Beyond that lay the village of Netherton, where she and her grandson used to live, and where her kinfolk were starving while still having to pay taxes to the Baron. "It's not their fault that they've got nothin' to eat," she continued hastily. "But dun yow lot care? No, yer don't!" Standing as erect as her aching back would allow, she adopted the stance of a preacher. "According to what the friars am tellin' us: the Bible says as the rich should give alms to the poor and needy. So what about giving 'em to your own poor and needy peasants? But no! All yow lot think about is—"

"Enough," cried the Steward, thumping on the table with his fist. He flopped down onto his seat and glared back at her in amazement. "*Cooks' bones*! I do not need a sermon from thee, old woman. You admit, then, to stealing those pies?"

"I would nay call it stealing," Jack's grandmother retorted. "It was just Christian charity."

The Steward shook his head. "Charity bestowed with victuals that did *not* belong to *you*."

"I made that pastry meself." She held out her flour-covered hands. "Look!"

"Using flour that belonged to the Baron!" said the Steward dismissively.

"That flour was milled from grain that was grown and harvested by the poor folks out there in the villages." She was pointing at the loophole. "Arr. And who are now starving for the lack of it." She snorted. "Yow as good as own 'em, but when did yow lot ever admit that yow has a duty towards 'em? Ay?" She gave a short ironic laugh to emphasise the rhetorical question. "Even peasants know better than to let their livestock starve to death."

The Steward flushed with anger. "If everybody helped themselves to our provisions, there would soon be none left. You may have heard, old woman, that we are at war with the Scots, and that the Welsh are threatening to take up in arms again. Every last crust is of value to us."

"But my lord," Gran protested, "them scraps was of no use to man nor beast."

"Ah-ha!" cried the Chef. "You have undermined your own case. Even scraps can be fed to the swine."

"Not all of 'em can't," Gran cried, still bridling at being called 'old'. "As I said afore: them crusts ain't fit for givin' to the pigs. The herbs as I put in 'em drives 'em mad. I should know. I gave some to my own sow once."

"So what use are they to your kinsfolk?" the Steward demanded. "Are their stomachs less delicate than those of swine?"

"Nay, my lord. But I told this boy..." She patted Zarn's bristly head, "to tell 'em to boil them crusts for a day an' a half, and then chuck away the water before eatin' 'em."

"Why?"

"Er... to kill off the moulds, o' course."

"Bring me those crustades," the Steward shouted to the guard standing by the door.

When the soldier had departed, the Steward fixed Gran in his worst stare yet.

"You have admitted to stealing food." He pointed an accusing finger. "By rights, I can have you drowned in the moat."

The old woman glared back at him, her arms crossed, her wrinkled lips compressed.

CHAPTER 3

The girl had remained silent while Gran protested her innocence of any crime. Now that it was clear that this had failed, she found her voice again.

"Spare them, Father," she cried, tightening her grip on his arm and wrenching him round to face her. "The old woman meant no harm, and she did nothing to her own advantage."

Before he could answer, the guard returned with the incriminating sack slung over his shoulder.

"Put it on the table," the Steward commanded. After loosening the string, he pulled out a crust and put it tentatively to his lips. "Ugh!" he spluttered. "You are right about this being unpalatable."

But despite that, it didn't diminish his opinion of the old woman's undoubted skill as a baxter. His mouth began to water at the thought of her delicious crustades – which were also greatly relished by the Baron – with whom he was *not* on very good terms at the moment.

The old woman stared back at him, feigning triumph but with terror in her eyes.

"In view of the circumstances," he announced, reaching for his quill, "I sentence thee to be placed in the marketplace stocks for... let me see... the rest of this day and all of tomorrow. In addition, you are fined a hundred silver pennies. DO NOT do it again!" He waved a hand dismissively. "Take her away," he shouted to the guard, who'd returned to the doorway. "But see to it that the stock-minder allows no throwing of bricks or stones. Tell him that if she receives even *one* cut or bruise, *he* will be the next to take her place." Grinning mirthlessly, he murmured to himself: "No doubt there are many who would appreciate the chance of getting even."

Feeling a sudden glow of self-satisfaction, his eyes sought out the urchin who was hiding behind the accused soldier's legs. Without deviating his gaze, he beckoned for the Chef to come closer. "See to it that the wretch gets something to eat before sending him back where he came from."

Still flushed with indignation, the Chef hustled his diminutive charge across to the curtain and both were soon lost to sight behind its folds. While the Chef could still be heard admonishing the sobbing child, the old woman's protests of innocence echoed up from the spiral staircase. Both disturbances faded, and soon could be heard no more.

The Steward now gave his full attention to Jack.

"As for you, soldier, you cannot deny your part in the theft. However," he added, mindful of his daughter's grip on his arm, "my daughter has pleaded for clemency."

"I meant no harm, Sire," Jack pleaded. "My grandmother said it would be all right!"

"All right?" scoffed the Steward. "All wrong!" He risked a quick glance at his daughter, whose eyes were brimmed with upwelling tears.

"He is still young," she sobbed, "and deferential to his grandmamma. That is good in a man is it not?"

"Very well," the Steward muttered. "I shall not involve the Sheriff in so paltry a matter as this."

As his daughter began to stammer out her thanks, he turned back to Jack. "I PRONOUNCE THAT YE BE STRIPPED OF YOUR RANK." In quieter but equally menacing tones, he added: "And exposed in the marketplace stocks alongside your grandmother. After that, you will spend the rest of your miserable life hewing limestone in the quarries."

"Please be more merciful," the girl implored, dropping to her knees beside her father's chair. The hound, who had been dozing in the warmth of the brazier, loped across to nuzzle at her groin. For once, she did not notice it. "Have pity on him for my sake," she cried.

The Steward rose unsteadily to his feet, his chair crashing backwards to the floor. Startled by the noise, the hound made a dash for the staircase door, almost upsetting the brazier in its headlong flight.

After righting his chair, the Steward seized his daughter by the arms and hoisted her to her feet. "What is this man to thee, Felicia? He is but a mere commoner."

Jack's heart swelled with pride. So the object of his adoration was named Felicia, and not only had she *noticed* him, she'd dared to speak up in his defence.

"WELL?"

Startled by the Steward's sudden outburst, Jack reached instinctively for his sword. Fortunately for everyone concerned, it was no longer hanging at his side.

"I just think that he deserves clemency," Felicia sobbed, "and the chance to make amends."

"He *deserves* to be beheaded – *twice* for daring to cast his impertinent eyes in your direction."

"But father, we have never spoken."

"Do not lie to me, my girl. Your eyes betray you both. TAKE HIM AWAY."

Immediately, Jack was seized and dragged across to the doorway. Impelled down the spiralling steps, he stopped himself from falling by jamming his elbows against the wall and the central pillar. But in spite of his despair and pain, his only thought was of Felicia. He could no longer hear her sobbing, even when the guard stopped taunting him to take a breath. Nevertheless, wonder and exhilaration swelled in his heart. *Felicia cared about him.*

As Jack disappeared from the hall, Felicia gripped her father's arm and turned him round to face her again.

"Be not so harsh, I beg thee," she sobbed.

"My daughter, it is in my power to send him to *the gallows* if I so wish."

"Please do not do that, father. He is so young."

"Felicia!" he growled, glaring down into her eyes. "You must see that I have no choice. Thieving our provisions is a serious matter. He has to be made example of to deter others from trying."

"But remember: it was *he* who helped you to flush out Lord Roger's killers."

"Yes," he admitted, carefully releasing his arm from his daughter's fingers, "for all the good it did."

"That was not *his* fault," Felicia protested. "It was the King's."

"Hush girl, lest anyone should hear thee." Nevertheless, he had to admit that she was right about that as well. Walter de Wynterton (the instigator of the murder) had been summoned five times to appear before the King's Justices. But he'd always failed to appear, and so was declared an outlaw. Then he'd turned up waving a pardon from the King, who supposedly held the Baron of Dudley in high esteem.

Resuming his seat, the Steward stared up at the smoke-hazed ceiling. His daughter stood quietly at his side, her hands clasped together in hopefulness... until her father's protracted silence became too much to endure.

"Well?" she blurted out. "You cannot deny that the King absolved Wynterton of the crime."

The Steward twisted round in his chair to peer into the dark recesses of the hall. Evidently reassured, he turned back to his daughter. "What you say may be the sooth," he whispered, "but unlike his father Longshanks, this Edward has little support from the other barons." He shook his head regretfully. "Taking advantage of that, Wynterton transferred his allegiance from Lancaster to the Crown. Rumour has it that he also gave the King a great deal of money." He gave a short ironic laugh. "Hung by the purse, as they say."

He hauled on his daughter's arm, forcing her to stoop so that he could place his whiskered mouth beside her ear. "My child, you are quite correct," he whispered. "Our so-called 'betters' commit the most heinous crimes with impunity. Nevertheless, I cannot afford to grant that soldier clemency, even for his much smaller crime."

"But LIFE!" Felicia screamed, tearing her arm away. "Does he really need to spend the *rest of his life* in the quarries?"

"Perhaps not, Felicia. With the Scots pillaging in the north, his skill at arms will be far more useful there. I might – *might* – be prepared to reconsider his sentence. But on one condition, mind."

"What is that, Father? I'll do anything. I shall even be nice to that horrid old man if it pleases thee."

"While that would please me *greatly*," the Steward muttered through gritted teeth, "the condition that I am demanding is that you do not speak to that young man *ever again*."

"But I've already told thee Father: I have not done so."

"If you promise to keep it that way, I shall commute his time in the quarries to… two months. That should still be enough to teach him a lesson that he'll never forget. It will certainly add more strength to his sword-arm." He smirked grimly. "However, I shall not let him know of it just yet. Let him stew in the stocks alongside his grandmother."

"Thank you. Thank you, father." After giving him a hug and kiss, Felicia dashed off to the curtain and was immediately lost from view.

As the Steward wiped his brow on the sleeve of his tunic, a servant appeared silently at his elbow. On a plate of polished pewter lay a red-ribboned roll of parchment, its seal embossed with the emblem of the King. Entrusted to open such missives in the Baron's absence, he prised off the seal and scanned the elegant script. It was another Royal Command for every town and village in England to provide a footsoldier for fighting the Scots. He grinned. That up-start young man was the ideal candidate for Netherton. Not only that, Will Hawkes would serve for Woodsitton. It was time that the forester paid for his laxity in not preventing Lord Roger's murder.

"Thus shall we rid ourselves of both of you at once," he murmured with satisfaction. While placing the precious document in his pouch, he heard a commotion beyond the lancet wind-eyes. Running quickly across to the nearest, he peered down at the courtyard below. The disgraced adults were being chained to the back of a wagon. The urchin sat rigidly erect beside its driver, awaiting his imminent return to the village of Netherton.

"That reminds me," the Steward muttered grimly to himself. "I still have to find a way of controlling the peasants while our soldiers are away fighting the Scots."

CHAPTER 4

Sitting side by side in the stocks, Jack and his grandmother made an unusual couple. The former wore a surcoat over his flour-encrusted aketon, but instead of sporting the Baron's blue lions, this one had a five-letter word painted on it in big black lettering. Fortunately for him, he couldn't read it.

The old lady had pulled her pinafore over her head to hide her shame. Nevertheless, the flour-paste on her skirts identified her as a baxter. Moreover, since baking was usually a man's occupation, she was well-known for being the only female pastry-cook in the area. It was also acknowledged that she was better at it than any man.

When they'd arrived in Dudley marketplace, the stock-tender was nowhere to be seen. Dragged from the nearby Man o' Leaves tavern, he was even less enraptured by the order to protect the prisoners from physical harm. Muttering his disapproval, he quickly installed the pair on the hard wooden bench and lowered the massive plank to trap them by their ankles. Unable to enjoy the sight of them being stoned, and forbidden to leave them to their fate, he consoled himself by swigging from a jug that he'd brought out with him.

It wasn't a market day, so there were very few people about. And those that *were* about showed no appetite for hurling missiles at the miscreants. Instead, they furtively scavenged the rotten vegetables that had been provided for the purpose.

"I'd have thought that you deserved better treatment than this," Jack grumbled, "after all that you've been doing for 'em."

"Don't be daft," Gran muttered from beneath her apron. "Once yow upset them in power, they'll never take yer past deeds into account."

With nothing more to say, they lapsed into uneasy silence, each with their own dark thoughts.

*

However, other folks had plenty to say on the subject. Word was getting round. As soon as Zarn arrived back home in Netherton, he'd gabbled out his account of events at the castle. And as his audience listened, their resentment grew – resentment at the treatment of their kin, added to the grinding injustices that were their daily lot. In no time at all, palms were being spat on and rubbed together. Staffs and pole-implements were being recovered from lofts and hayricks. A leader was being elected, and a plan of action agreed.

*

For the pair imprisoned in the stocks, the rest of the day passed with agonising slowness. The tradesmen soon packed up and left, while Jack eventually tired of chiding his gran for her stupidity. She no longer felt the need to justify her actions on the grounds that "the nobs chuck away more food than they ever eat." And as the sun disappeared behind the houses on their right, they both grew increasingly reluctant to speak.

Before them towered the preaching cross, reproaching them for their sins. From there, the High Street sloped up to Top Church on its hill. The thatched roofs on their left were bathed in gold while those on the right were clothed in darkening shadows. Behind the wind-eyes of the Bailiff's house nearby, candles were being lit and an evening meal prepared – its aroma adding torment to discomfort.

Jack's grandmother was the first to break the silence.

"It's a good job this is summer," she said, leaning sideways to ease a buttock from the hard, unyielding timber. "Even if they leave us out here all night, we shall come to no great harm."

"Speak for yourself, old woman," Jack groaned. "I need a pee."

"Take no notice of me," Gran muttered. "If yow'm that desperate, just get on with it. In any case," she added with a smirk, "you've nothing that I have-nay seen afore."

While quivering with suppressed mirth and embarrassment, they heard shouting in the vicinity of Top Church. Down the High Street towards them galloped a horse – the cart behind it ablaze with burning hay. Bright flames streamed out along both sides, and a cloud of spark-flecked smoke billowed in its wake. The church bell chimed the alarm: *Save... the... thatch... save... the... thatch.* Men with grappling-poles scurried up the street, anxious to pull down any straw that had caught alight. Others headed down towards the Horsepool, their iron buckets clanking as they ran. And all this while, the horse with its blazing cart careered towards the miscreants in the stocks. Veering round the cross, it passed the captives by in its headlong flight. They glimpsed the whites of the poor beast's eyes as it sought to escape the inferno close behind, which had already singed off its tail.

With no wet clouts to protect their mouths and noses from the fumes, Jack and his gran had fits of violent coughing (during which Jack wet himself). But as he cursed his gran for the umpteenth time, a tapping sound rang out in the murky darkness.

"The stock-keeper's lighting his lant-horn," Gran said hoarsely.

"I'd never have known!" Jack retorted with a sneer.

After one loud blow that was heavier than the rest, shadowy figures emerged through the swirling smoke. The heavy wooden plank was hauled up from the prisoners' legs. Strong arms were lifting them to their feet and dragging them away down a narrow and winding passageway. By the time the smoke had thinned to a wispy mist, the miscreants were nowhere to be seen.

*

"Where am you a-takin' me?" Gran dug in her heels and pushed back against the hands that impelled her forward. A man in the lead pointed further down the slope.

"See that?" he said. "Yow'll be safe there." Beyond a field of spindly corn, a well was roofed with thatch to keep out dust and bird droppings.

"Yow want me ter go down *that*?" Gran screeched, aghast. "I shall drown."

"You'll not even get yer feet wet," someone murmured quietly in her ear.

Gran turned to see who it was that was shoving her along. A slip of a girl grinned back with sheepish eyes.

"But the Devil lives under the ground," Gran protested. "Everybody knows that."

"Even if he does," the leading man said with a chuckle, "we've never seen 'air nor 'ide of 'im yet."

"What about evil spirits then?"

"There's none o' them neither. Well, apart from our own evil spirits that is – seein' as we'm so angry and bitter about not havin' nothin' to eat."

Not at all convinced, Gran allowed herself to be hurried among the cultivated strips.

"What's that for?" she wailed as they neared the stone-built wellhead. Instead of a bucket, a plank-seat dangled down from the windlass drum. "That's a *ducking stool*. I ain't no witch."

"We don't care if you are," a woman whispered. "But keep yer voice down. We don't want nobody to hear us."

Gran stared with horror at the gaping hole.

"There's no need to worry, missus," said a man at the winding handle. "It's quite safe."

"*There you are, Gran.*"

She turned to find herself staring up into her grandson's dark brown eyes.

"Jacob," she cried. "Thank the Lord. I've been praying that they'd be bringing you along as well. Look, they want me to go down there."

Together they watched the seat swinging over the shaft.

"Me too," Jack muttered grimly. "They say that it's the safest place around." He reached out and grabbed the seat. "You go first, Gran. The hue and cry will have been raised by now, and the posse could well be right behind us."

Muttering under her breath, Gran allowed herself to be manoeuvred onto the seat, which Jack had carefully placed on top of the parapet. The crank began to turn. To rattle of clicks from the ratchet, the rope was wound slowly onto the windlass drum. Gripping the two that were digging into her shoulders, Gran was hauled up from the parapet, her legs scratched by the stonework as she swung backwards over the shaft. Amazingly, no protest came from her tight and wrinkled lips. The ratchet being released, the windlass reversed direction, gathering speed as the tensioned rope unwound.

As Gran vanished behind the parapet, her expression changed from one of bitter resentment to another of barely-controlled terror. The crank continued to turn until the rope went suddenly slack. Clicks from the windlass ratchet announced that the seat was on its way back up. It arrived empty. It was Jack's turn now, and he needed no cajoling; he could hear the cries of their pursuers in the distance. If they got their hands on him now, they would probably chuck him headfirst down the shaft.

CHAPTER 5

With Jack being so much bigger than his gran, it was quite a squeeze to get past the windlass winding-drum. Urged on by the distant cries of his pursuers, he gladly allowed himself to be lowered into the well, the speed of his descent being much greater than Gran's. Cursing the pain as his elbows scraped the wall, he could hear the trickle of water far below. They had told Gran that she wouldn't get wet, and they were right. Strong hands reached out to haul him to one side, and then deposit him down on solid ground. The opening of a lant-horn flap revealed that he was standing in the entrance to a tunnel. His gran was sitting on a box beside two men, both in dust-covered clothing, with their knees protected by leather poleyns.

The man nearest to the shaft tugged on the rope, whereupon the seat rose swiftly and silently out of sight.

"What is this place?" Jack asked, leaning out to follow its progress up the shaft.

"We dig the sea-coal here," the second man answered proudly, "and send it out to our families when the Bailiff isn't looking." He turned to Gran. "See for yerself, missus: there's no evil spirits down here." He chuckled. "Though there *are* some good ones. There's pure water for drinking, and along there..." He rotated the lant-horn so that its beam shone down the tunnel, "there's fuel for warmth and cooking."

Gran made no reply. The rough-hewn timbers that held up the roof looked far from safe.

"Come along," said the lant-horn carrier as he headed off down the tunnel. "They are waiting for us."

Confused by this strange turn of events, Jack followed him down the passageway, stopping only to support his gran when she tripped up on the rubble. He'd long-since chucked away his incriminating surcoat, and his aketon was adding coal dust to its crust of hardened flour-paste.

The tunnel sloped gently down, following a seam of sea-coal whose facets sparkled briefly as they passed. Balks of timber shored-up the roof – although occasional heaps of rubble showed where they hadn't. After what seemed an age of stumbling along in the dark, the lant-horn carrier announced that they were nearly there. Gran looked past him and shrieked.

"I thought you said as there was no evil spirits down 'ere?"

In the cavern that opened out before them, a single candle revealed a crowd of unearthly beings. Crouching on spidery limbs, they looked about ready to spring. For faces, they had skulls, and within the dark eye sockets, glowing points of light glared in her direction. As Gran turned to make a run for it, the lant-horn carrier gripped her by the arm.

"They'm here," he cried, his words echoing back from unseen walls. "Let's have a bit more light so as yow can see 'em clearly."

The single candle spawned another. Then there were four. Then six, then twelve. The growing light revealed just commonplace men: thin and haggard but not at all frightening now. Most were sitting on limestone boulders that had obviously fallen from the unsupported roof. In front of them stood an older man who seemed to be their leader.

"Come on in," this Leader cried, turning to greet the newcomers. "It's good to see thee." After scrambling over the rubble, he seized Jack's hand and shook it with unwarranted vigour. "You'm just in time."

"Just in time for what?"

"Just in time to help us to fight for our rights. We've heard that you'm skilled with the weapons of war and we want yer to show us how to use 'em." He turned back to face his men. "Don't we, lads?"

As the cavern boomed with roars of agreement, Jack peered around unwillingly.

"Fight?" he said. "What with?"

With a wave of his hand, the Leader indicated a row of farming implements that stood propped against the wall of the cavern. Their straight white staves contrasted brightly with the irregular grey surfaces of the rock.

"You intend to fight the castle garrison with *these*?" Jack marched self-consciously over to the makeshift armoury and seized one of the implements with both hands. Its five-foot pole was surmounted by a sickle-like blade. Turning to face his audience, he made a couple of sideswipes, intending to demonstrate its unwieldiness as a weapon. But it wasn't. It was lighter than a battleaxe and more versatile than a spear. "This is not bad," he announced with unconcealed astonishment. "The balance is good. You could certainly bring down a mounted knight with this, but you'd have to get close enough to use it first." He shook his head regretfully. "The men at the castle have bows of Spanish yew. They would strike you down before you could get anywhere near them."

"WE have bows as well!" The Leader nodded towards another stretch of wall, where a thicket of unstrung bows leaned against the rock. "We are skilled with *them*, at any rate."

"I don't doubt it," Jack said. "But if you tried to attack the castle, you would be shooting uphill against stone walls. *They*'ll be shooting down through arrowloops and crenels, er… battlements – while *you* will be out in the open."

"We can knock up some of them pavise shields."

"They would simply knock 'em down. Remember, many of those soldiers have fought alongside Longshanks in Scotland. They've driven off sieges by Bruce's entire army." Jack replaced the slashing-implement against the wall of the cave. "No," he declared, "I shall have none of it. It would be suicide."

"You have no choice," the Leader bellowed. "Our bairns are starving to death. Our wives cry themselves to sleep cradling the thin little bodies in their arms. And we …" He waved an arm at the sullen multitude, "can no longer stand the pain."

Seeing Jack's blank expression, he spat, "What would *you* know? By the look of yer, they've been feedin' yer very well up there in the castle." He turned to Gran with desperation in his eyes. "But *you* know what it's like, don't yer, missus?"

"I know right enough," she answered sadly. "We've been through it all afore."

"Even so," Jack cried, "attacking the castle will only make things worse."

As the chamber reverberated with murmurs of disappointment, the Leader sprang forward. A dagger glinted in his bony hand.

"You WILL help us," he snarled, "or you will never leave this place alive."

In one swift movement, Jack retrieved the implement from the cavern wall and swung the head at the back of his attacker's knees. At the very last moment, a twist of his wrists reversed the blade so that only the blunt edge struck home. The man's legs buckled under him and he went down like a skittle.

THWACK! A lump of stone bounced off Jack's encrusted aketon. But as he congratulated himself for having retained its protection, a second stone bounced off his forehead and everything went black.

Jack awoke to find his wrists and ankles bound. His head was aching. There was uproar in the cavern.

"Let me go," he screamed, horrified by the discovery that he hadn't been having a bad dream after all.

"So you've returned to us at last!" the Leader cried. He raised one hand for silence and seized Jack's grandmother with the other. "So *are* you willing to help us? If you don't, you'll never see daylight again."

"It would do you no good," Jack cried, struggling to free himself. "Even if I *did* train you to wield those weapons, you would never be strong enough to face the castle's garrison. And what are you going to do when they defeat you? Have you thought of that?"

Once more, the cavern resonated with angry murmurs.

"We *have* thought of that," the Leader shouted. "If the worst comes to the worst, we shall all clear off to Barnsdale, or even *Share*-wood. We've heard that the outlaws up there have carved out nice little kingdoms for themselves in the forest."

Gran turned on him. "Do you think those wolf's-heads are going to welcome more hungry mouths to feed?" she cried scornfully.

"Why not?" replied the Leader. "We've heard that they've slaughtered so much venison that they can share it with the poor."

"But how d'you intend to get there," Jack protested, "with the Baron's men hot on your heels?"

"The Old Park will cover our retreat," the Leader said dismissively. "And next to that lies Hampton Wood. Then it's only a short march to lands controlled by Lancaster. Once there, we shall be beyond the Baron's reach."

"Oh ar?" Gran shouted. "And what about your women and babbies, not to mention the old 'uns like me? Goin' ter take 'em all off into the woods are yer? I thought the whole idea was to keep 'em safe from harm."

As the cavern erupted with confusion, she tugged on the Leader's sleeve. "You'm goin' about this the wrong way."

Yanking his arm away sharply, the Leader rounded on her. "Dostow have a better plan?"

"Look!" Gran turned to address the crowd. "I know that your families are running short of fittle. My own folks are having to eat weeds and dried berries until this year's corn has been got in. And we know that *this* year's harvest is going to be even worser than last year's." She nodded her head in the supposed direction of the town. "We could see *that* on the way down here."

"And your point is?" cried the Leader, folding his scraggy arms across his chest.

"My point is that them at the castle rely on *yow* lot to reap the corn for 'em. And unless yow *do*, there'll be no bread for them to eat... nor for their precious army for that matter!"

The cavern hummed with murmured conversation.

"So you are suggesting *what*, exactly?" demanded the Leader.

"I am suggesting that yow refuse to reap this year's corn until the Baron agrees to issue you with some food."

In the flickering light of the candles, gleaming eyes stared back in pensive silence.

"We should *refuse* to reap the corn?" the Leader murmured in amazement.

"Ar!" Gran cried, warming to her theme. "They did it in a village over to the east of here. A tinker told me about it. They handed in a petition."

"And what happened?"

"Believe it or not, the lord of the manor eventually caved in and granted their wishes. After all, he wasn't stupid."

"And were there any reprisals?"

"A few," Gran admitted. "They had to pay a hefty fine, and the women had to do extra work on the lord's demesne lands while the men had to train as his foot soldiers." She waved her hands to quell the grumbles of discontent. "But they would have had to do *that* anyway, with the Scots laying waste to the north of the country!"

Still trussed up and lying on the rocky floor, Jack considered his position. If he refused to cooperate, he would almost certainly be killed. They would probably do the same to his gran (and serve her right, the silly old crow). And yet he knew for a fact that revolt would be a disaster. He was almost as dubious about the peasants downing their sickles. Either way, he could see himself having to flee the district with them. And even if they *did* manage to reach 'Share-wood', how would they be received? With drawn bows, most probably. In spite of what the balladeers were singing, according to barrack-room gossip, Robin Hood would sell his grandmother for a penny. Jack glanced across at his gran and the sight of her stopped him dead. She was staring at him with wide-eyed expectation.

He glared back at her in horror. "You want *ME* to present these men's case to the Baron?"

"Who better?" she cried, nodding furiously. "You could get their petition writ by the monks in the Priory."

From the roar of approval that filled the cavern, it was clear that the men were in full agreement. Obviously, each of them had been terrified of being selected for the task.

"And who better to be hung from the castle battlements!" Jack shouted, turning his face away to hide his fear.

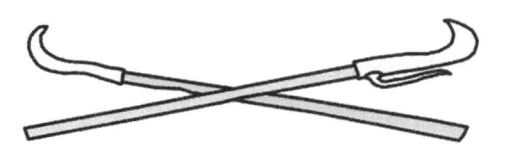

CHAPTER 6

Jack lay back among the rocks of the cavern, refusing to consider his grandmother's suggestion. "It will be certain death if I represent these men," he protested.

"Nay lad," his Gran replied. "*Ore corn-trair*, it's the only chance of saving both our skins."

She turned to face the men who sat pensively in the candlelight. "I know what I'm a-sayin'," she cried. "I keep me ears open, especially when there are nobs about."

In the ensuing silence, each pair of ears strained to hear what might be forthcoming.

"So!" she announced at last, "I expect as you've heard that the Earl of Lancaster has been trying to bring this king of ours to account." As the murmurs resumed, she raised her voice just enough to remain audible. "Well, they say as there's going to be a big bost-up between the two of 'em, and that it ain't clear which of 'em's going to come out on top. Our Baron must be messing himself in case he's on the losing side."

"What's that to us?" cried a voice from the crowd. "One bad master is much like any other."

The crowd agreed.

"Oh no it ain't!" Gran cried. "Yer might think that John de Somery is bad, but Lancaster's supporters could be much worse. But as I was *about* to say: our Baron is well aware of what's been happening on his manor." Surprised murmurs filled the cavern. "Oh yes!" she screamed. "He's got spies in all the alehouses. Yer dain't know that, did yer?" She paused, as if waiting for an answer. "Well he *has*," she continued, "and he knows how desperate yow lot'm gettin'. Ar! And he won't have taken kindly to having to leave fighting men behind in case you *do* decide to attack his precious castle."

The cavern became hushed as its inhabitants digested this information. It was so quiet that you could hear a drip drop!

The old woman turned to her grandson. "So Jacob," (she knew that the name would goad him) "the Baron should be grateful that you're offering him a way of using his men to the best advantage."

"NO!" Jack screamed. He was getting panic-stricken now, for he could sense that these men were all behind her – *willing* him to agree.

Placing the palms of her hands on two adjacent boulders, Gran lowered herself gingerly down between them.

"Good grief," she muttered. "These rocks am agony to me poor old knees. Roll over here will yer?"

Reluctantly, Jack obliged. While wiping the blood from her grandson's forehead, Gran whispered into his ear.

"Listen. This might even get you into the Steward's good books."

"How d'you make that out?" Jack whispered back.

"Well. Just before the Baron went off to support his King, I had to take some of his favourite crustades up to the donjon. Of course, I had to use the servant's stairs. Then I had to wait behind that curtain 'til the Baron and the Steward finished talking. That's when I heard the Baron making the Steward responsible for any disorder in the manor while he's away. Not only that, he told him that if there *was* any disorder in the manor – any at all – he would find himself hewing limestone in the quarries. And the best of it *is*, that judging by the Steward's tone of voice, I am pretty sure that he's got no idea how to go about stopping *disorder in the manor."*

Aware of her grandson's thoughtful silence, she added fuel to the fire. "And if I'm right about that, he might look more favourably on you wooing his precious daughter."

"What was *that?*"

"I've got eyes in me head as well as ears," Gran said with a wink. "I've seen the way that you look at her. Ar! And I've also seen her watching *you* when yer wasn't looking."

He was weakening. He could feel it. Life without Felicia would be no life at all. Just to be able to see her occasionally would be enough to keep him going, whatever the future might hold.

"But as soon as he lays his hands on me," Jack groaned, "he'll have me thrown into prison … or worse."

Even as he was speaking, he guessed that there would be a counter to his objection. There was.

Gran struggled painfully to her feet and turned again to the men. "He's worried about his safety," she cried.

The Leader hurried across to his prisoners. "Yow can claim sanctuary in the Priory. The Steward cannot touch you there – well, not for forty days at least. That's easily enough time for you to deliver our petition."

"But what will happen to me after *that*?" Jack screamed. "How will I get away?"

"You may not *have* to leave the Priory," replied the Leader. "If you learn a few words of Latin, you can claim to be a trainee monk." Ignoring Jack's incredulous expression, he explained himself: "Then you'd be subject to Monks' Law only and outside the Baron's control." He shrugged. "And even if you *did* have to get out, you have the advantage of being on good terms with the Forester of the Old Park. Will Hawkes would surely help yer to escape. By the way, the Prioress of the Black Nuns has offered to give us shelter if we ever need it. It is not far from Brewood to lands still controlled by Lancaster, and he's always on the lookout for more trained fighting men."

So that was it, then! Jack had no alternative but to go along with his grandmother's wild scheme. That left him with just two options: after getting the petition writ and delivered to the castle, he could make his escape as soon as the opportunity arose. But what should he do then? He didn't fancy joining the outlaws up in 'Sharewood' (wherever that was). But what was the alternative? Enlist in Lancaster's army? The way things were going, he would end up fighting his mates from Dudley Castle. And he couldn't switch sides like De Wynterton. Somehow, he doubted that *he* would be granted a royal pardon. He was more likely to get a sword up the backside for his pains.

The second option was to try to become a monk. Even if that *was* possible, the conditions that he'd witnessed at Hales Abbey held no appeal. In any case, what could he offer the Priory? His prowess as a fighting man? That might not be such a daft idea after all. The monks were bitterly resented. They might be grateful for somebody like a Templar to protect them. He might even see Felicia from time to time. After all, he'd heard of monks visiting women of the town.

All right then! He would do it. When it came down to it, he had very little choice.

Part Two

Priory

CHAPTER 7

On one dark and particularly stormy night, a dozen or so men crept stealthily from the well. Jack emerged last. After his hands had been tied behind his back, he was led into the shelter of a nearby yew tree. From its thrashing branches, tattered strips of fabric streamed out in the wind – hung there as rippling invocations to the ancient gods.

Crowding round their Leader, the men urged him to abandon his chosen route across the town. They had to admit that it *was* the shortest way to get to the Priory. However, the Bailiff could be lurking among the houses – ready to pounce on any reckless soul who dared to ignore the curfew. And here were *many* such reckless souls, daring to risk it in the hope of staving off their family's starvation.

"He ain't the only problem," somebody cried. "We'll never get across them streams."

There followed a roar of almost unanimous agreement, although this was barely audible in the tumult all around.

The founder of the settlement (which bore his Saxon name) had chosen his site wisely. For although it occupied the saddleback ridge between the castle and Top Church, five springs lay within easy reach of the houses. All fed streams that had swept away their bridges, having become swollen into rivers by the rains. The only one on this side could be heard roaring past in the darkness, barring their way to the route around Castle Hill. That left only a detour of Top Church.

"All right. All *right*," the Leader admitted at last. "Have it your own way. But that means entering farming lands that belong to the Priory.

Have any of you been down there lately?" Hearing nothing but the howling of the wind, he shrugged. "Me neither. So don't blame *me* if we run into the monks in the darkness."

"What?" yelled a member of the company. "In *this* weather?"

"We could ask 'em to take Jack back with 'em," suggested another.

"An' then we c'n all go home," cried someone else to murmurs of accord.

That decided, they abandoned the limited shelter of the yew. With the rain congealing the dust on their cloaks and hoods, they hurried along between strips of bedraggled corn. Giving the church a very wide berth, they crossed the Sturbrugge Road unseen. Then by slinking up stony paths between more strips of battered-down crops, they came at last at the high road that led to Hampton.

So far, Jack had remained silent, his mind a chaotic muddle of doubts and fears. While the Leader hesitated at the road's edge, he realised that this might be his only chance of escaping. After all, his captors were weak from hunger and he was strong and healthy. If he took them by surprise, he could surely fight the lot of 'em single-handed. They probably knew that too, although they gave no sign of it.

However, they must have been aware that he wouldn't escape while his gran was still held prisoner down that well. As she herself had pointed out, they could never let her go if it all went wrong. So it was up to him to ensure that the plan succeeded.

"Why have we stopped?" he yelled in the Leader's ear. "It's freezing cold up here."

And so it was. With the wind being funnelled up the vale that lay before them, they were now exposed to the full driving force of the storm.

"I'm not sure where we are along this road," the Leader shouted back, the liripipe of his hood lashing wildly in the wind. "Should we go straight across or look for someplace better?"

"What's wrong with *here*?" Jack bawled, struggling to make himself heard above the howling gale. "We could get through a gap in the hedge."

The Leader moved up closer. "Four streams run down to the Priory from below this road." His breath smelt repulsive in spite of the air that streamed between them.

"What of it?" Jack said as he turned his head away.

"Only one arrives there. They must all meet up on the way down. We could get trapped at one of the junctions, and arrested if the Bailiff is coming after us."

"You think that we're being followed?"

"We might be. Not everybody wants us to risk upsetting the Baron."

"I know of one stream that should be safe to follow." Jack's shout was scarcely audible in the storm. "I was taken across it as a boy."

"Arr!" bellowed a shadowy figure on his right. "We've heard about that hunting party."

The Leader nudged Jack's painful elbow. "Did the Baron treat you well for killing his brother's murderer?"

"You must be joking," Jack answered grimly.

"What have we stopped for?" cried someone further down the line. "We ain't got all night."

"Keep yer hood on," the Leader yelled back.

Jack turned back to him. "That stream forms part of the Old Park's boundary. It goes nowhere near the Priory, and feeds the Baron's corn mill at the bottom of the vale."

"He's right," somebody shouted. "That's so's the monks can't staunch its flow in times of drought."

"Not much chance of that," cried someone else to shrieks of hollow laughter.

"As I was saying," Jack croaked, his voice now hoarse from shouting, "All we've got to do is find the Old Park's boundary."

The Leader could now assert himself once more.

"Follow me," he bawled, pointing up the road towards the distant town of Hampton. "The top part of that boundary borders this road."

"As if we dain't all know that," a voice cried out in the wildness.

Ignoring that remark, the Leader set off briskly up the road – well, as briskly as anybody *can* who's tugging a reluctant prisoner while being blown sideways off his feet by a howling gale.

It took a long time to reach the Old Park's boundary and then to follow it down to Jack's remembered stream. With the wind now blowing fully in their faces, they kept their hoods pulled down against the rain. By keeping the roar of the stream on their left-hand side, they descended with growing confidence into the vale. That confidence soon gave way to doubt and frustration as their boots suddenly filled with ice-cold water. They had wandered into the stream in the darkness. But whichever way they went, the water showed no sign of shallowing. All four streams must have burst their banks – flowing down together in a broad cascade.

Cursing his rotten luck, the Leader splashed off down the slope again, tugging on Jack's tether as though he were a mule. Jack stumbled over a tussock and sprawled full-length in the swirling, freezing water.

"We can't go on like this," he yelled, hauling on the rope to struggle back to his feet. "If I promise not to escape will you untie me?" He didn't need to promise it, and his captor knew it too. After only a moment's pause, the Leader untied the soaking bonds.

"Don't you forget that you've given me your word."

They set off again, the Leader probing the water with the heel of his staff. Jack splashed along behind him, urged on by pricks from a pitchfork in his back. The other men followed in single file, squishing and swearing in the tumult of the storm.

A flash of lightning tore across the sky. It vanished as quickly as it came, leaving behind a darkness more profound than ever. A clap of thunder made Jack jump, arriving much sooner than he had expected. Extending the first and fourth fingers of his right hand, he pointed them at the sky and muttered the age-old prayer to the old god Thunor.

"What's this?" the Leader shouted, stopping in his tracks. "Artow afraid of thunder? Have we picked a coward for our spokesmon after all?"

"I am *not* afraid," Jack protested. "That bolt struck home shortly after it was released. Thunor's chariot isn't far away and he's heading in our direction." Relieved that his embarrassment was hidden by the darkness, he added: "That prayer has always kept me safe before."

"Yer don't believe in that old wives' tale?" the Leader scoffed.

"Well the *'old wife'* in question," Jack shouted back angrily, "just happens to be my grandmother. And you've heard for yourself that she's no fool." The refutation sprang unbidden from Jack's lips, surprising himself even more than it did his critic. But before the Leader had the chance to answer, a second bolt of lightning cleaved the clouds, accompanied by an instant crash of thunder.

"I told you so!" Jack yelled, crouching low and gesticulating frantically. "He's up above our heads. The monks must have summoned him here to stop us."

If he had hoped that this observation would cause the Leader to abandon their mission, he was to be disappointed. Another bolt of lightning flashed, revealing a patch of drier ground nearby. The crack of thunder took its time arriving.

"Thunor's ridden past now," the Leader cried with a hint of relief in his voice. "So yer c'n relax now."

Relax? Jack couldn't relax. Here he was, forced to take part in an increasingly hazardous venture with very little chance of it succeeding.

Taking advantage of successive flashes of lightning, the Leader steered a course down to level ground.

"Halt!" he cried, stopping suddenly and jabbing backwards with his elbow when Jack didn't.

"Sorry," Jack muttered, and then cried out as the pitchfork pronged his back. "Your Leader said *HALT,*" he bellowed to his tormentor. No apology was expected, and none forthcoming. Instead, he heard the command passed back from man to man as each obeyed.

"We've come to the Priory fishponds," the Leader shouted.

Jack passed that back as well, each man relaying it to the one behind:

"We've come to the Priory fishponds."

"The Priory fishponds."

"Fishponds."

Finally becoming just "Ponds" as it reached the last man in the line. They had come to a halt on a muddy stretch of pathway. With the wind somewhat abated, Jack listened to the hiss of the rain lashing unseen water. Another flash of lightning lit it up clearly. Although it vanished in an instant, it had etched a gleaming image in Jack's mind.

Through slanting streaks of raindrops seemingly frozen in their falling, the fishponds stretched away on either hand.

Beyond them lay the Priory, its mottled silvery stonework rising straight up from the water. On the left, a buttressed wall had a row of tiny wind-eyes along the top. On the right, a gabled frontage enclosed one large impressive wind-eye, pointed at the top like an upturned shield. Immediately below that, a similarly-shaped arch framed the entrance to the Priory. With a squat, square tower at the rear, it seemed to be built for defence rather than for Christian worship. And it all contrasted starkly with the dark and looming bulk of Castle Hill, upon whose crest an ice-bright faerie fortress rode the sky. Jack had been to the Priory before, when the Baron brought his brother's corpse for burial. But on that one occasion, he'd been much too scared of getting an arrow in his back to take much notice.

The mental image faded, leaving just that single wind-eye glaring out into the rain.

"Didst ow see that doorway over there?" The Leader's hand alighted on Jack's cold shoulder. "It's underneath that wind-eye."

"I saw it," Jack replied, "but how are we going to get over there?"

"Not 'we' – *YOU*."

Jack shrugged him off, angered by his offhand manner. But as the man headed off along the pathway, Jack grabbed *him* by the arm.

"There's something lying in the water."

"What? Where? Is it a boat?"

"Back along the bank. I think it's a dead body."

As if in confirmation, the Priory's bell began a mournful toll.

For the first time since the journey began, the Leader opened his lant-horn's flap. With the horn plate kept in place to shield the candle from the wind, the light that it gave was feeble and tinged with green. Nevertheless, it revealed the stationary figure of a man lying face-down in the rain-lashed, seething water.

Soon they had him out on the bank, with the Leader squatting down and feeling for a pulse.

"He's dead," he announced as the death-knell ceased abruptly, "but he's still warm."

This was an understatement. He wasn't just warm: he was positively *roasting*. As the raindrops thudded down on the inert body, puffs of steam shot up into the air to be whisked away on the wind.

Trying to ignore the spittle flooding his mouth, the Leader rolled the body onto its back. Glazed eyes stared up accusingly at the sky that had struck him dead, for his fist still clutched a length of twisted iron. "He must have been fishing," the Leader announced as he prized the rod from charred and blackened fingers. Using the rod as a makeshift prop, he hauled himself back up to a standing position.

Murmurs of sympathy ran along the line, for each of Jack's guards had poached to feed his family. One now voiced the question that all were thinking:

"Why should Thunor strike him dead for stealing from *Christian monks*?"

"Perhaps Lord Yay-sous borrowed Thunor's chariot," another suggested.

"And used his bolts to kill a *fisherman* like his disciples?" cried the first. "That don't seem right to me!"

"He could have sent Thunor out to do His bidding," came the petulant reply.

"And the monks must have prayed for this to happen," a third man added as they all stared down at the dead man at their feet.

"I *knew* there was sommat queer about them monks!" somebody yelled. That final comment drew roars of pensive agreement.

"Queer or not," the Leader cried, "that's of no interest to *us* as long as they help us with our petition."

"And grant me asylum," Jack shouted quickly.

"Oh arr!" admitted the Leader after a moment's hesitation. "That an' all."

"So how are we… er… I… going to get across?" Jack asked.

By way of an answer, the Leader directed his lant-horn beam further along the shoreline, revealing only windblown rushes.

"There's a causeway further along there," he barked as he snapped the lant-horn shut.

A flash of lightning showed it in the distance. Heading arrow-straight across the lake, it ended at the high and buttressed wall. The lychgate straddling the approach was where the black-robed monks had taken charge of Lord Roger's body.

When their squelching arrival brought forth no challenge from within, the guards shoved Jack inside and crowded round him in the damp and dripping darkness. Sheltered from the rain, they bent their hooded heads to his, reminding him of the purpose of his mission – as if he needed any such reminding. Once satisfied that he'd fully understood, they tugged their bows from tubes of well-waxed linen and bent them to receive their uncoiled strings. The hissing of the rain had turned to pounding as it thrashed the shingled roof above their heads. By the light of successive flashes of sheet lightning, Jack watched as arrows were nocked... drawn back... and aimed in his direction.

His shoulders hunched, he slouched to the other doorway, the slowly-moving target of deadly shafts. He had no fear of arrows in his back just yet. These knaves would wait until he'd carried out what they wanted – or failed in the attempt. Nevertheless, those arrows conveyed the message: there was to be no going back for him.

CHAPTER 8

With the wind tugging ceaselessly at his cloak and hood, Jack stared out into the black tempestuous night. How the hell had he got into this situation? Having been falsely accused of stealing from the Baron, he'd been released from the stocks by this band of knaves. Forced to leave the safe shelter of the well, he'd been pelted with ice-cold rain, blinded by Thunor's bolts and deafened by their thunder, and then yanked over to fall face-down in muddy water. Now he was in the 'lychgate of the dead', having to dash across a muddy causeway in the storm. To what? More whistling monks?

He couldn't come back to the lychgate – that was clear. These knaves would surely kill him if he failed to present their petition, and then they'd have to silence his gran as well.

"I'll just wait until this cloudburst passes," he yelled, still staring out into the darkness.

Another flash of light lit up the causeway. Fringed with thrashing reeds, it led straight across the lake to the buttressed wall – whose right hand end hid the entrance doors from view. Were they going to open and let him in?

Turning to face his abductors, he yelled back at their shadowy figures: "You surely don't expect me to go out in *this*?"

The Leader moved up close in the musty darkness. "You can't leave it much longer. Dawn is not far off."

As Jack recoiled once more from his stinking breath, the Leader went back to confer with his waiting men. Grumbling with displeasure, one by one they crept out into the night.

"Where are they going?" Jack yelled, foreseeing the probable answer.

"They've gone to surround the moat."

A lightning flash revealed the Leader clearly – his bow fully drawn and an arrow aligned unwaveringly on Jack's heart.

"Careful," Jack cried. "With that wet glove on, the string could slip off your fingers."

Conceding the point, the Leader slackened his bow. Holding the arrow against the handle with the thumb of his left hand, he cast aside the other hand's soaking glove. For one wild instant, Jack thought of trying to rush him. But the man drew back the bow with naked fingers and Jack had missed his chance again.

"It's time for you to go," the Leader announced. "And don't even *think* of trying to escape. You will not slip through our cordon, that I promise you."

The pounding on the roof had lessened slightly. The wind was easing and the lightning flashed less often.

"I hope the monks will be more hospitable than you," Jack yelled. "Don't wait up for me."

Head held down, he dashed out into the storm. Slithering around puddles, he skidded across the causeway, the water boiling and bubbling on either side. He managed to get across without slipping in. Turning sharply right, he followed the buttressed wall, its wind-eyes frowning down beneath brows of dishevelled thatch. The wall turned left, then right to merge with the high and gabled entrance to the Priory.

Now standing on a muddy cobbled forecourt, Jack gazed up into the rain. Bright light blazed out from the wind-eye high above him, tinting the falling raindrops with changing colours that vanished before they splashed down on his face. Some of that light shone back into the archway, revealing a pair of massive oaken doors. Wrought iron bands spiralled across their planking, close enough to thwart all but the smallest axe. The place really *was* built like a fortress, with not a single wind-eye within reach of the ground.

Resentment seethed within Jack's heaving breast: resentment of what that building represented – a haven of protection for a bunch of foreign monks while all around them Englishmen were starving. Breathing deeply to steady his nerves, he tried to drive the bitterness from his mind. He needed the monks' protection for himself.

In the middle of the right-hand door, a lion's-head knocker held a ring in dripping jaws. Jack raised this up and let it fall against its stud. The impact sounded duller than expected, but at least it shouldn't have carried across the lake. Nevertheless, he peered round at the further shore. Although it seemed deserted, his former guards would be hiding among the bushes. They would not leave until he'd gained an entrance. An arrow struck the door beside his head, bouncing off to slither across the cobbles. It was only a blunt, but the meaning was only too clear: Get inside those doors or we're going to pin you to them.

Jack huddled against the timber, hoping to find some shelter beneath the arch. He didn't find much shelter, but he *did* find a patch of wood that was clear of ironwork. With his ear pressed to it, he held his breath and listened, hearing only the splashing of raindrops on the cobbles.

He knocked again – this time ramming the ring down on the stud. The impact sounded louder, but still there came no acknowledgement from within.

What should he do now? Wait until the monks felt like getting up? He could easily catch his death out there in the rain. A few yards back the way he'd come, the lee-side wall offered some protection from the wind. He raised the knocker for one last thump, but something stayed his hand. As well as the squeak of the ironwork, he'd heard somebody's whistle. He carefully lowered the ring. Had he imagined it? No. There it was again. Too loud to have travelled across the lake, it seemed to have come from the other side of the doorway. But there was no one there, and the footprints in the mud were all his own. He felt the gaps between the wood and the stonework. They were all too narrow to have carried that piercing sound. So the Priory really was haunted as folks claimed… by the ghost of a whistling monk.

As fear added further chill to that of the wind and rain, he made a dash for the corner of the walls. But with his hood pulled down to shelter his face, he collided with a hitherto unnoticed buttress. And as he cursed and rubbed his painful shoulder, a third whistling sound shrilled out beside his ear. Between the archway and the buttress, a block of stone was missing. He peered into the hole that was left behind. Glowing with flickering light, it clearly pierced the yard-long thickness of the wall. Somebody inside was trying to attract his attention. Leaning over the batter at the bottom of the wall, he put his mouth to the tiny tunnel. He took a deep breath... then breathed it out again. Too loud a shout might attract unwelcome attention. When a second anxious search confirmed that there was no one else in sight, he returned to the hole. With the hems of his hood pressed against the uneven stonework, he called inside as loudly as he dared:

"Is anybody there?"

"Who's that?" The voice from the hole sounded foreign and distinctly hostile.

"My name is Jack."

"Art thou alone?"

"Yes," Jack answered impatiently. "And standing out here in the rain."

"Wait there while I confirm that with our lookouts."

The light grew dim and then went out. The hole now reeked of hot fish stew, transporting Jack back in memory to Hales Abbey. He'd been taken there as a boy for his own protection, since he alone had seen Lord Roger's murderer. Now here he was again, seeking refuge in a holy place; but this time *from* the Baron.

"Art thou still there?" The voice from the hole catapulted him back to the present. Before he could answer, the voice continued: "What dost thow want from us?"

The cavity was flickering with candlelight once again.

"The villagers want to send a petition to the Baron," Jack answered hurriedly. "Can't you speed this up for g-g-Goodes' sake?"

"So why hast thou come *here*?"

"To get it put down in writing."

The doors resounded with the bangs of bolts shot back. The door with the knocker swung back on groaning hinges, and no sooner was the gap wide enough, than Jack was through and shaking raindrops off his cloak.

CHAPTER 9

"About time too," Jack muttered as a monk closed the door behind him. "I was beginning to think that you were never going to let me in."

"Young man," the monk said curtly, "there are more important things than answering doors to the likes of *you*."

The cleric wore a habit of thick black cloth. A wreath of silver hair encircled his pate and a frost of silver stubble covered his chin. A belt of knotted rope held up an ample paunch and a bunch of heavy keys swung from his hand.

"God bless thee my son," he said with unconcealed disdain. "You are welcome to stay here with us for one day and night."

"Only one day?" Jack shrieked. "That's no good to me. I want to claim sanctuary here."

"And why is that, pray?"

Just in time, Jack stopped himself from blurting out that he was on the run from the castle. The monks might be prepared to offer him shelter, but like everyone else within the manor, they relied on the Baron's patronage. Their allegiance (after God) would be to *him*.

"Why d'you think?" he screamed. "There are people out there who want to kill me."

"Be quiet," the monk commanded in an urgent whisper. "We are a silent order here. Thou wilt either respect our customs or be ejected." He jangled the keys to emphasise the threat. "Which is it to be?"

Jack almost laughed in the old man's face, being young and strong and in his prime. However, he contented himself with muttering: "But *you* are talking."

The monk shrugged. "I do so as the Porter here. Nevertheless, I speak only when it is really necessary. And even then, I take great care not to disturb the sanctity of this holy place."

And a holy place it undoubtedly was. Beneath Jack's puddling feet, a chessboard pattern of red and black tiles stretched away to a carved and gilded screen. Atop that gaudy barrier, a golden cross glowed brightly in the flickering light – for along the plastered walls, serried ranks of candles lent restless life to glittering scenes of angels fighting devils. The air hung heavy with the conflicting scents of molten wax and incense. High magic was at work here.

The monk led the way to a small wooden cell on the left side of the doorway, the soles of his shoes slapping softly in the silence. Jack slouched along behind him, his soaking boots sounding more like slimy slithering.

"If I promise not to shout," Jack said as the door clicked shut behind him, "shall I be allowed to stay here?"

"Only the Prior can decide that," the monk said casually. "And not until Lauds is over."

"You are expecting the lords?" Jack wailed. "The kinfolk of the Baron?"

"Be *quiet*," the monk growled. "If you cannot be silent, I must insist that you leave." He toyed with a rope that dangled against the wall. "I have only to tug on this to summon assistance."

"I'll be quiet," Jack mumbled.

"Stay here then while I get thee some dry clothing. And for your information, 'Lauds' is the service that we hold at dawn each day. That's L, A, U, D, S."

Jack waited, idly turning the pages of a book that lay open on the table. He couldn't read a word of it.

"That's none of your business," the monk snapped as he scuttled back in through the doorway. He held a thick woollen garment, washed to mottled greyness by many years of service. A snow-white towel was tucked beneath his elbow.

"Sorry," Jack said, trying to force a smile.

"Speak only when thou art spoken to," the monk commanded, ignoring Jack's outstretched hand. "I'll take those wet clothes from thee first."

Glad to get rid of his cold and soaking garments, Jack dragged his hood off with one hand while unfastening his cloak with the other. They plopped together onto the floor. His jacket, tights and pantaloons followed suit, leaving him standing naked in his boots. The priest kicked the soggy bundle into a corner and handed the towel over. Jack wiped himself down as quickly as he could, turning his back to avoid the other man's blatant stare. He'd seen that same expression in the alehouses, as the boozers watched the barmaids bend to the barrels.

With his back still turned, Jack dried his sensitive parts – remaining that way as he handed back the towel. Only then did the priest relinquish the monkish robe. Jack hauled the garment over his head and let it fall around him. The coarse woollen cloth rasped against his skin, both heightening and concealing his embarrassment. When he'd recovered his composure, he turned to face his benefactor. Moving up close and staring Jack straight in the eyes, the monk encircled his waist with a length of rope.

"I welcome thee in peace," he murmured while tying a simple knot. Then he kissed Jack on the lips.

Jack dashed for the door, the hairs on the back of his neck springing free of their bonds of sweat and dampness. When he'd got there unmolested, he risked a glance over his shoulder. The monk was kneeling down in silent prayer, fingering the knots in his belt and ignoring Jack's existence. To distance himself from his unwelcome admirer, Jack scuttled towards the carved and gilded screen, his slopping footfalls echoing back from the plastered walls. What had he let himself in for now? If all the monks were like *that* one, the sooner he got out of there the better.

Flanking the screen, fluted stone columns rose against the side walls before curving over to meet above the cross. From a doorway below it came the sound of muted praying. When a waist-high gate prevented him going further, he leaned across to see what lay beyond (after an anxious glance behind).

In chapels leading off on either side, carved figures of knights lay flat on grey stone boxes, all but one with a lady at his side. So *this* was where the nobs came when they died. The lone one had a clean and fresh-cut look; its shins encased in greaves instead of maile. If that was meant to be Lord Roger, the face was not a bit as he remembered it.

While these effigies had their hands pressed together in prayer, the voices came from a chapel straight ahead. Framed by two more fluted columns, it stretched away to a second great shield-shaped wind-eye. On an altar below, crucifix, goblet and flagon gleamed with the unmistakable sheen of polished silver.

Resplendent in the light from a seven-branched candlestand stood a life-sized statue of a man cast in solid gold. Looking nothing like the statues of Lord Yay-soos, its robe reached down to the floor like those of the clergy. Folds and embroidery had been copied by a master craftsman – one far more skilled than the sculptors who'd carved the ladies lying so stonily beside their lords. These monks possessed immense wealth while people outside were starving.

Jack was turning away in anger and disgust when a movement caught his eye. The statue's arms were spreading like golden wings. It beat them together in time with the rhythmical praying, and rose slowly into the air. There it was – hovering like a great big glittering sky-mouse; a foot at least above the polished tiles. And all around it, strands of gold streamed out in restless motion.

He rubbed his unbelieving eyes and looked again. It was still there, as large as life and a hundred times more beautiful. There was no doubt about it. He was looking at an angel. So they *did* exist after all: the beings that he'd thought were just priest's tales, and no more real than Woden's nosy ravens.

He hugged himself, thrilled at being in the presence of a heavenly being. The priest at the castle had admitted to never having seen one. Presumably, *he* wasn't considered worthy enough. Jack flushed, feeling far less worthy than a priest. As far as his gran was concerned, he was one of the wickedest people to walk God's earth.

Kneeling down on the cold hard tiles, he hung his head in shame. Shame for all the trouble he'd caused his gran; shame at how he'd resented running her errands – often spinning a knife to ensure that his journeys would be fruitless – and shame for other sins now long forgotten.

How was *he* to know that Gran had been struggling to keep him warm and fed while she herself went cold and hungry? She'd even been keeping his clothes aired beneath her own. No wonder she'd got painful knees and elbows now. Jack prayed for forgiveness in silent faltering words, while watching the heavenly being with half-closed eyes. His sense of outrage returned. Why should an angel be bestowing God's blessings on a bunch of foreign monks, here in the middle of poor old downtrodden England?

Of course! The nobles always claimed that God was on their side. How else could they have conquered the whole of the country? They'd probably built priories like this to give thanks for services rendered. He grimaced. So *that* was why they called their prayer meetings 'services'.

Brushing away his tears of sadness and resentment, Jack watched the heavenly being with less enchanted eyes. The golden strands had vanished now, but a pointed crown had leapt up onto its head. As Jack struggled with the conflicting feelings of reverence and anger, the angel turned and stared in his direction. It knew that he was there – profaning that holy place. Still beating its wings together, the angel rose higher off the ground. It was about to come flying down the aisle and drive him out.

Jack looked around in panic. Even if he *did* reach the entrance doors, he'd never get hold of the key. Retreating to the side wall, he backed against the buttress. Amongst its flutes was one that moved. It was only a cup-topped pole for dousing candles, but it would do as a makeshift weapon. He wasn't prepared to go down without a fight. Twisting off the cup to expose the pointed pole-end, he shuffled his boots to ensure of the firmest footing. Breathing deeply, he stepped out to meet his doom. The chapel held its stony breath, awaiting the impending confrontation. The pictures on the walls were about to be re-enacted in real life... with *Jack* in mortal conflict with an angel. Twenty pounding heartbeats passed with agonising slowness, and still the angel had not come. Jack glanced fearfully up at the top of the screen, expecting to see the angel perched up there – ready to pounce and tear him limb from limb.

It was not there. It was not there. Backing again to the fluted ribs of the buttress, he waited... waited... waited, and still the angel did not come.

Perhaps it was not coming after all.

He risked a peep through a gap in the gilded screen. The angel was still hovering in the chapel, but now it had its back turned towards him. Jack hadn't noticed before, but along both sides of the chapel, black-robed monks were standing in the shadows. *They'd* been doing the praying that he'd been hearing, although it had stopped and he hadn't been aware of it until now.

A heavenly voice echoed down the aisle. It was male, but not entirely masculine. It was singing, but not like any singing that he'd ever heard before. The words were clear, but clearly not in English; they sounded like those that the priest used up at the castle. So Latin really *was* what they spoke in Heaven.

The melody was not really a tune at all. The notes were all sung at the same level pitch, before rising or falling at the end of every other phrase. Each time the voice fell silent, the choir of monks repeated its refrain, their voices adding volume to the hymn. And so the litany continued – alternating between the single voice and the chorus of the choir – wafting the sacred words up into the rafters and beyond – and carrying with them all Jack's hopes and fears.

The singing changed abruptly – becoming a wall of sound, built up with layers of constant but differing pitch. With the notes fading in and out at regular intervals, it was quite some time before Jack realised what they were singing.

"Alley... loo... yah. Alley... loo... yah. Alley... loo... yah," repeated over and over in soaring waves of sound.

A gentle peace flowed over him, the like of which he'd never felt before. Kneeling down again, he bowed to the Almighty... 'til another nagging thought sneaked into his mind. Could they be summoning up a spirit to smite some sinner? Somebody like that poacher in the lake? *Somebody like himself?* And as this disquieting thought occurred to him, something thumped him heavily on the back. He sprang up and round, an 'Alleluia' dying on his lips. A hooded figure towered over him – vast in stature and black from head to foot. The angel had not come for him in person. It had sent this devilish being in its stead.

The devilish being raised an arm to point like a gibbet to the doors that led outside. Cold sweat broke out all over Jack's trembling body.

Stepping back and to one side, he lunged with his makeshift spear. The being swung its arm – striking the pole from Jack's hands to send it slithering over the tiles. But as he turned to retrieve it, he felt himself held back by a powerful force. With fear and trepidation, he turned to face the horror at his side.

CHAPTER 10

From the shadowed interior of the hood, a pair of gleaming eyes stared into Jack's own – but not from the skull-like face of the angel of death. This face was human, with at least a full week's stubble on its chin. Shrugging off the hands that held him by the shoulders, Jack snatched a quick glance through a gap in the nearby screen. He could no longer see the angel, and the chapel was growing darker as the candles were extinguished one by one. Without a word, the giant seized Jack's arm and led him towards the exit doors. But just before they reached them, he veered off to the right – to a small pointed door that Jack hadn't noticed before. The giant flipped its latch and forced it back against the wind that came surging in.

"Shut that door," came the cry from the Porter's hut opposite. Jack smirked. So much for his claim of always keeping quiet. Invited to go out first, Jack lurched down a step that the giant hadn't bothered to mention. The meagre light vanished as the door slammed shut behind them, but not before Jack had glimpsed a pair of covered walkways. Ignoring the one in front, the monk turned right and headed off down the other. Jack crept along behind, hugging the uneven stonework of the chapel and besplattered at regular intervals with unseen spray. Eventually, the passage turned abruptly left to where a narrow strip of light revealed a door that was partly open. The giant knocked once and stood aside for Jack to enter.

*

A dark-eyed monk looked up from his desk and half-arose from his seat. Like the other brethren, he wore a robe of black woollen cloth.

In contrast to the others, his features looked thin and drawn. A smile flickered briefly across them, vanishing so quickly that it could have been a wince. Jack hesitated, dithering in the doorway, until beckoned to come inside and take a seat. The priest resumed his own and, resting both elbows on the table, placed his fingertips together in a prayer-like attitude. By staring over them at Jack's clenched fists, he made it clear that he should to do the same. The priest then bowed his head and Jack did likewise. The priest began to pray, making no sense at all to Jack, until the tone of his voice signalled an imminent end:

"In Noh-mi-neh Pah-tris et Fee-li-ee et Spee-ri-toos Sanc-tee." With a final "Arr-men," the priest looked up and gave Jack a meaningful stare.

"Arr… men," Jack mumbled, wondering why they always said: '*Yes Men*'.

"So how may we be of service to thee, my son?" the priest asked quietly.

In hushed and respectful tones, Jack began by relating how the crops were failing and the people who relied on them were starving.

"I *do* have some inkling of *that*," the priest announced, his eyes cold and humourless.

"The villagers want a petition sent up to the castle," Jack carried on quickly, "to beg for enough food to see their families through to the harvest." Seeing the priest's questioning look, he added lamely, "But none of them can write."

"And does that include thyself?"

Jack blenched, ashamed of his inability. "That's why they sent me here to get it written down proper."

Described out loud, his mission seemed even less likely to succeed. Nevertheless, he continued with his well-rehearsed speech until forced to take a breath. He had more to add but the priest's raised hand forbade it. "So why did they not inform the chief tithing man?" he asked coldly.

"Nobody trusts him. He would report them to the Bailiff."

The priest frowned, apparently considering the situation. When next he spoke, he adopted an even more suspicious tone.

"Our Porter reports that you came here on your own. Is this the sooth?"

"That's right," Jack said, startled by the change of subject.

"So *who are those armed men who've taken up position round our fishponds?*" The priest's manner had deteriorated to barely suppressed hostility.

"They're some of the villagers I was telling you about."

"Then why have they surrounded us?"

"They're just making sure that I don't escape. While I'm in here, I can't betray them to the Steward."

The priest leaned back in his chair, seeming more relaxed. "So how camest thou to get involved with them?"

"I lived with some of 'em in Netherton. But they still aren't sure if they can trust me or not."

"And can they?"

"I suppose so. Anyway, I have no choice but to do what they demand. They are holding my grandmother prisoner to make sure of my continued cooperation."

"Very well," the priest announced. "I am prepared to let thee stay here for the time being. By the way: how did they manage to free thee from the stocks?"

"By driving a fire-wagon down the..." Jack stopped himself in mid-sentence, but too late. The priest had tricked him. "So you know who I am," he muttered bitterly.

"It wasn't hard to guess. And where is the baxter now?"

Jack sat silent and confounded. The game was up. Or was it? The priest was still fishing for the truth. But revealing any more could get him into even more trouble. Nevertheless, the Priory wasn't the right place for telling lies.

"I cannot tell you that. If I did, you'd probably inform the Bailiff and then they'd kill her."

"So how came *she* to be punished in the stocks? Canst thow tell me that at least?"

"She gave away some stale crustades."

"She gave away some *crustades*?" He smiled that little smile again, his eyes still narrow and mistrustful. "If they were as stale as you claim, wherefore was the harm in that?"

"That's what *we* thought," Jack said hastily. "Unfortunately, the Steward did not see it that way."

"That explains why *she* was in the stocks, but not why thou wert with her."

"She got me to help her," Jack said simply.

The priest shifted uneasily in his chair. "I see. And was there any profit in it for thee?"

"None at all. But when our kinfolk begged for help, how could we refuse?"

"If what thou sayest is the sooth," the priest murmured thoughtfully, "thou wert following the teachings of our dear Lord. I think that such a deed deserves our recognition." Reaching for a quill and a scrap of parchment, he scribbled a brief note. "Here," he said, handing the document over. "Take this round the cloisters to the Scrivener. I grant thee thy petition." He smiled his vanishing smile once more. "And I shall affix the Priory's seal to show that it has our blessing."

"Thank you my lord," Jack said, glancing at the writing and understanding nothing. "And are you going to grant me sanctuary here as well?"

"Not so fast, young man. There are three conditions to be met."

"*Conditions?*" A chill of apprehension ran down Jack's spine.

"First," the priest intoned, "I require assurances from your accomplices that they will leave us—"

"They will not bother you," Jack interjected hastily.

"...and resume attendance at Holy Church."

"But I thought that everybody had to do that," Jack protested. "It's compulsory."

"They seem to have given up the practice."

"But I can't make 'em."

"Nevertheless, that is my condition."

"You want me to go out and tell 'em, then?"

"Nay. No one leaves the Priory while there is so much unrest in the town. And as I said: I have more conditions."

I'll bet you do, Jack thought – more conditions than a lame, blind leper.

"As the next condition," the priest announced, "I want a regular supply of your grandmother's crustades to be sent to me here in the Priory."

"How can she bake crustades when she's imprisoned down the well?"

"So *that's* where they're hiding her," the priest declared triumphantly.

Jack stared down at his hands, horrified by his carelessness and disconcerted by the craftiness of his inquisitor.

"Well of course," the priest continued, "that's *after* she has been returned to the castle, which is part my third condition."

"She mustn't be handed back," Jack wailed. "As soon as the petition has been presented, they'll think that she's in league with the rebels."

"Oh all right then," said the priest with a heavy sigh. "I shall just have to get my crustades from the Steward if he's got any left. That's a pity!"

"Anything else?" Jack asked, amazed to hear of the Steward's secret dealings.

"I think that's all for now." The priest leaned forward. "Upon thy acceptance, I am prepared to grant thee forty days' sanctuary here, but only if you obey Saint Benedict's Rule."

"That's *four* conditions," Jack said sharply. "You said there were only three."

"Saint Benedict's Rule applies to *everybody* here. Myself included." He gave that short-lived grin, or was it a grimace? "It's a general rule."

"What *is* this... Saint Benny Dick's Rule then?"

"There are several of them. For instance: thou art not to speak to the brethren unless thou art spoken to first. And thou must attend prayers in the chapel at least thrice daily."

"Three times a day?" Jack echoed, aghast.

"That is what we expect from all our visitors. The brethren pray seven times a day."

"That doesn't leave 'em much time for getting into mischief," Jack muttered, remembering the Porter's behaviour.

"Why dost thou say that?" The priest had looked up sharply.

Jack remained silent. An outright accusation was unlikely to be well received.

"WELL?"

"No particular reason," Jack muttered, still trying to banish the doorkeeper from his mind. In the hope of changing the subject, he added lamely: "I don't know any of your prayers. That's all."

"Thou wilt soon learn. And we have plenty of hymn sheets."

"Are they all in Latin?" When the priest nodded his confirmation, Jack reminded him: "I can't read English or French, let alone *Latin*."

"Well, do thy best. That is all we can expect."

Jack had a sudden thought. "I've been told that if I *do* learn some words of Latin, I can claim to be a member of this priory. Then you could let me stay here, and they couldn't prise me out."

"That will not be possible," the priest said wearily. "That would put thee outside the Baron's jurisdiction. I assume that thou hast sworn allegiance to him? Yes? Well! He would not tolerate it."

"So what happens when the forty days are up?"

"Then shalt thou leave us."

"To take my chances outside?"

"That's right!" said the priest, thrusting back his chair and rising from his seat. He seemed taller now, but slender-boned and wiry. "There is just one act to be accomplished." The priest reached down a bowl and a pitcher from a shelf behind him and placed these on the floor beside Jack's chair. After kneeling to remove the sodden boots, he lifted both feet into the bowl and emptied the pitcher over them. Shocked by the icy immersion, each foot in turn succumbed to expert kneading. Jack allowed his gaze to wander round the room. The floor tiles were not plain like those in the chapel. These were decorated with De Somery's pair of lions – reminding him to be careful of what he said. As if it wasn't too late for that. Apart from the desk and two chairs, the only other furniture was an iron-bound chest in the corner. The rear wall was filled with shelves, all but the lowermost crammed with books and piles of folded parchment.

Jack peered down at the man still kneeling beside his feet. If this really *was* the head man of the Priory, it was a head man who was not averse to demeaning himself before a stranger – one who could be a mass-murderer for all he knew. If only this man could be persuaded to let him stay.

"Could I offer my services as a mercenary?" The words had slipped from Jack's lips without a moment's forethought. Not for the first time, he wondered if someone else was present in his head. "After all," he added self-consciously, "there are plenty of violent people out there."

The priest gave no sign of having heard – engrossed as he was in drying Jack's feet on the hem of his robe. "We have received thy mercy, O Lord Jesus," the priest intoned, "here in the midst of this, thy holy temple." After emptying the bowl back into the jug, he returned them both to the shelf.

"What happens now?" Jack asked as the priest turned back to face him.

The monk pointed at the parchment in Jack's hand. "Just tell the Scrivener what thou wouldst have him write."

"But you said that I'm not supposed to speak to anyone unless they speak to me first."

"This will be an exception. Brother Michael will escort thee round the cloisters to the scriptorium. Speak quietly so as not to disturb the peace." Scooping up Jack's boots, he strode briskly over to the doorway.

After exchanging words with the monk outside, he stood aside for Jack to take his leave. But as Jack reached the door, he halted open-mouthed.

CHAPTER 11

Down the back of the door hung a robe that was different to all the others. In spite of being shaded from the candles by Jack's body, it glowed more brightly than their lustrous flames. Fine gold wires had been woven into cloth of the same illustrious colour. Recognition hit him like a blunt arrow on the head. The man at his side was none other than the 'angel' in the chapel. There had been no heavenly visitor after all. Hoping to find some flaw in that conclusion, Jack studied the garment closely. In spite of the wires and the closely-woven fabric, its style was not unlike his own ganache. His gran had bought him that woollen garment to protect him from winter's cold.

He lifted up a sleeve and held it out. It *could* look like a wing when seen from a distance. But without any wings, how had the wearer risen up into the air? By magic? The garment's length was also the same as his ganache's – reaching to just a few inches below the knee. With a black robe underneath, *the wearer would appear to be hovering in the air.* Shocked by the realisation, he allowed himself to be hustled out through the doorway – where the giant monk was waiting with patient resignation.

Jack had been having cold feet all night. Standing barefoot on damp and chilly flagstones, he didn't think they'd *ever* been so frozen. Where were his boots? The giant monk hadn't got them.

Forbidden to speak, Jack pointed down at his feet and hopped from one to the other a couple of times. Sniffing at this sacrilegious prance, the monk turned on his heel and marched off down the cloister.

Now that Jack had been promised that he could stay, he took more interest in his new surroundings. Just visible in the gloom of that reluctant dawn, four rows of arches framed a square-shaped central garden. Scuttling after his guide, he caught glimpses of various herbs through successive archways. Most of the plants were sagging beneath the downpour, while the nearest lay flattened by the run-off from the roof above his head. Nevertheless, he recognised some that his gran had used when she'd been the wise-woman of Netherton. Well she *hadn't been very wise when she gave those crustades away*.

His anger evaporated as he approached the end of the cloister. Where it turned abruptly left, a youth stood leaning into the corner. His arms were extended, his palms pressed against both walls. The skirts of his habit were girded to his belt, revealing a bum that was scarred but thankfully clean. Jack stopped and stared, forbidden to ask the reason. While he stood there open-mouthed, an older monk came hurrying towards them. His sleeves were rolled up, a whip twirled in his hand, and a sadistic smile played upon his lips.

Jack had to leave them to it, for his guide was marching off along cloister number three. Catching him up, Jack tugged on his sleeve. Together they looked back to where the youth was being soundly thrashed. And not just 'soundly'; it was 'soundlessly' as well. Not even a groan escaped from the young man's lips.

The giant monk shrugged and carried on walking, to a buff stone trough that was standing against the side wall. Here, Jack was 'invited' to wash his hands and forearms. Finding comfort in the lukewarm water, he pondered on his impressions of the Priory.

At first, he'd felt amazement and awe, swiftly replaced by outrage and resentment. Lord Jesus had told his followers to give their wealth to the poor and needy. As one of the poor and needy himself, Jack had always been greatly impressed by that commandment. But while the poor and needy of Dudley were starving around them, these monks in their fortress were sitting on a hoard of gold. The most shining example of that had been the 'angel' in the chapel. He grimaced at the thought of his gullibility. But for one brief, glorious moment he'd actually *believed* that what the priests were saying was true. This had not been the half-hearted acceptance that stole over you as you listened to a long and tedious sermon. It had been full-blown absolute *certainty* – proved by what he was seeing with his eyes. But since it hadn't been an angel after all, his doubts had returned even stronger than before.

He swirled the water around in his agitation, his knuckles scraping on a roughness on the bottom of the trough. As the water became still, a strange little fish-like creature stared back with unblinking eyes.

"Hello little chap," he whispered quietly. "What are you doing here?"
"Shhhh."
The monk was glaring at him.
"Keep yer hood on," Jack said. "I was talking to the fish, not to you."
"That was left behind by Nower's flud," the monk stated flatly. His belligerent expression had been replaced by one of smug devotion. Jack felt his own change to one of scepticism. The monk's complacency got him riled. He prodded the little creature with a finger. It was as hard as the rock in which it lay entombed. He'd seen similar things in the limestone blocks of the castle, alongside shells that presumably once lived in water. It was hard to believe that Nower's Flud had been the downfall of them all. He'd also seen petrified fern fronds in the sea-coal down that well. That rock was black, while the other two were yellowish-brown and white. No! The monk had got it wrong. There had to be a better explanation than The Flud[1].

However, the priest up at the castle preached that such things had been created by a tempter he called '*De-Evil*', to undermine people's faith in the Holy Scriptures. That *did* make sense. After all, the thing that he was looking at now had given rise to his own doubts and uncertainties. So the Devil had been at work all over the manor, even in this, the holiest place of all.

"*Seeing is believing.*"

Jack breathed in sharply. Those words had just appeared amongst his thoughts. Where had they come from? Who had sent them? Or what? And why? It happened quite often, as if somebody was putting alien thoughts in his mind. He'd had them most embarrassingly in the presence of full-bosomed women, and the priest had declared that those too were the work of the Devil.

---

1 Proved by the Royal Society's expedition to a Dudley coal mine in around 1603.

"He's right," Jack murmured, relieved to have found an excuse and an explanation. *That* was who had been whispering in his ear. A foot below the surface of the water, his reflected face stared back with fearful eyes. He swirled away the image with his hands – afraid of seeing the Devil peering over his shoulder.

"And about time too," the giant monk snarled as he offered a clean white towel. "Now I've got to take you to the Scrivener."

A short distance down the cloister, a shutter was closed and bolted against wind and spray. The monk rapped on a door beside it and ushered Jack inside. Beeswax candles filled the air with welcome warmth and fragrance, as well as providing bright and shimmering light. Seated behind a desk, the Scrivener sat rubbing his eyes with ink-stained fingers. In front of him lay a foot-square sheet of parchment, on which a border of painted vines enclosed rows of neat lettering. Jack presented his note and waited for some reaction.

"You can see that I'm busy," the Scrivener muttered icily. "You can dictate your message when I've finished transcribing this page." Sucking in air through pouting lips, he stooped to rummage in a box beside his feet. When he eventually straightened up, he was holding a pair of tallow candles. Into each of these he thrust a pin at two inches from the wick end. Then, igniting both candles from one of his own, he stuck them onto large blocks of wood. One he placed down on his desk, and the other he gave to Jack. By the look of the candle's diameter, he was in for a lengthy wait.

After expressing his thanks, Jack joined his monkish guide beside the door. But as the latch was lifted, the door flew open and crashed against the wall. A gust of wind swirled in, flurrying parchments and blowing out all but one of the candles – the survivor having been shielded by a wooden frame covered with vellum. Silhouetted against the film of glowing calfskin, a quill pen span in its pot as though demented. Apparently remembering its former role in life, it twirled up into the air. The Scrivener made a grab for it, but missed. It hovered above the manuscript, whirling like a sycamore seed while scattering whorls of ink-spots over the writing. As the giant monk slammed the door, the pen dropped like a dart down onto the document, the impact splaying its tip like a fledgling's gape. The Scrivener stared in horror.

"*Sigil*," he gasped, reaching for the cross that dangled on his chest.

"What's 'Sigil'?" Jack asked, ignoring his vow of silence.

"It's the sign of the *Devil*." The monk lifted the shade from his candle to see more clearly.

Jack's heart missed a beat. He'd been thinking about the Devil and there was his sigil: an inkblot shaped like a bearded head with horns. The cramped little room was unbearably hot. He had to get out. And fast.

"If you light my candle," he said, banging its block down on the desk, "I'll go away and leave you in peace."

When the Scrivener paid no heed, he plonked it down again.

"What was that?" the cleric whispered, still staring at the blot.

"My candle needs relighting," Jack repeated.

The monk turned to look at him as though seeing him for the first time.

"Very well," he said, shaking his head as if to clear it.

Tutting like a blackbird alarming danger, he ignited Jack's candle and did likewise for its twin. After pausing for a moment, he moved both pins down by half an inch. "I must first clear up this mess," he said while taking a pinch of sawdust from a box and sprinkling it over the parchment. "Nevertheless, I should be with thee by the time thy pin drops out." He picked up the shade and plopped it over Jack's candle. "This will keep the wind off in the cloister. Be careful with the door as you go out."

Although the giant monk *did* take more care when opening the door, a gust of wind surged past him into the room. The quill pen now embarked on a flight of self-cremation, and as the door was closing, the Scrivener's coughs could be heard through the narrowing gap. Ignoring the aroma of hot fish stew, the giant monk led the way into the fourth leg of the cloister, with the doorway to the chapel straight ahead. But it wasn't the one that they'd come out of; *that* had a pointed red stone arch instead of the level lintel that Jack was looking at now.

His mind searched frantically for an explanation. Since this was a different door, could the cloisters be spiralling him up to a higher level? He'd heard of 'Jacob's Ladder' going up to Heaven. Was this an other version, with the cloisters forming a ramp winding up into the sky? But if that *was* the case, he'd have seen it from across the lake. What was he thinking of? That idea was stupid. A glance through a nearby arch confirmed it. Nothing out there had changed. The cloisters were all joined up. The puddles were all unflowing – so the garden was still flat. Yet he knew that he wasn't mistaken about that door. As with the 'angel' in the chapel, he could conjure up its image in his mind. One thing was certain: if he wasn't already crazy, he would be by the time his forty days were up.

"Where do you think you are going?" The giant monk had called from several paces back, his hand on the rail of a narrow flight of steps. "It's up here."

The stairway took them up to a lean-to attic that was even more depressing than the cloisters had been below. The headroom being restricted, they were forced to bow their heads beneath wooden shingles, all rattling like little drummer-boys demanding attention.

The monk reached for the candle. "I'll take that now. We don't want another fire."

They proceeded in the same direction as before, their heads confined to the wedge-shaped space where the roof sloped up to meet the sidewall. With the light of the candle largely hidden by the body of his escort, Jack felt his way along that wall, hemmed in by racks of candles on his left.

A thought crept into his mind. The monk had mentioned a fire. If he needed to create a diversion, he could set these candles alight. He grabbed a couple as he crept past, but having nowhere to conceal them, he had to put them back a bit further along. Halted by the blank wall of the chapel, the monk shuffled round in the slightly larger roofspace. With his shadowed face grotesque in the light of the candle, he nodded at a doorway at his side. Jack gaped at the hefty padlock gleaming there. He'd hoped to have found a refuge, not a *prison*.

CHAPTER 12

The monk produced a key, jammed it into the padlock's slot and grunted as its staple released the hasp.

"You're the first one to stay in here for ages," he said as the door swung open into a dark and silent room. With the candle held out in front, the monk led the way inside. Jack took a step forward, tripped over the threshold, and fell heavily against his back.

"Watch it," the monk roared, rounding on him angrily. "There's no need to hurry. You'll be spending a lot of time in here from now on." After sniffing the air, he opened up a shutter and fastened it with its stay. The lancet wind-eye faced down the wind, allowing in light and fresh air but hardly any rain. Through it came an all-too familiar sound: the relentless spatter of raindrops splashing on cobbles. Jack rushed across and peered outside and down. Below him lay the entrance to the Priory.

Now that he knew where he was to stay, Jack surveyed his new abode. A room about seven yards square had more religious paintings on the walls, but without the gold embellishments of those in the chapel. Opposite the door, three small shuttered wind-eyes must be those that frowned down from the top of the buttressed wall. Immediately below their embrasures, wooden beds held palliasses sheeted over with smooth white linen.

"Does anybody else sleep in here?" he asked, receiving a shake of the head to indicate a negative.

Jack grinned with relief. Not only did he have the room to himself, it was nothing like the cells up at the castle. In fact, it was better than the room that he'd been sharing with his fellow guards. But if this wasn't to be his prison, why did it have a padlock on the door? Was it to stop monks sneaking in for a snooze? Well, if that included the Porter, perhaps that lock wasn't such a bad idea after all. But what if the *Devil* appeared and he couldn't get out? He might be able to squeeze through that lancet wind-eye – though it must be at least fourteen feet down to the ground.

By swinging his gibbet-like arm from side to side, the monk announced that Jack could choose his bed. He picked the one that was closest to the lancet wind-eye, hoping to keep watch for visitors from outside. The monk now raised his hand for Jack to stay, then took his leave and shut the door behind him. There came the snap of the hasp folded back, and the rasp of the key withdrawn.

After making quite sure that he'd been locked in, Jack ran to the farthest corner of the room. The wind-eye there would be the closest to the lychgate; he could show the knaves out there where he was staying. Hauling the bed out of the way, he flung the shutter back and braced it against the wind with the iron stay. Through cascades of water streaming down from the thatch above, he looked in vain for the causeway and its lychgate. But with the wind-eye being so small and the wall being so thick, all that he could see was a featureless stretch of the shoreline. Leaning into the embrasure didn't help; the buttress on its right restricted the view. He'd intended to use the candle to show where he was staying, though he'd have to stand well back to avoid the draught. So even if someone *was* out there and waiting for a signal, they'd have to be dead in line in order to see it. Was there anything else to use? The bedsheet would do even better. After dragging it off, he held a corner of it out into the rain – waving it from side to side like a flag of surrender. A speck of light flashed out from the bushes opposite, and vanished as the lant-horn flap was shut. With the bedsheet now wrapped loosely round his forearm, he beckoned for the watcher to come across and parley. Eventually growing tired of what proved to be fruitless waiting, he closed the shutter and returned to his lancet wind-eye. Using his bedside table as a seat, he settled down to watch the doors below.

No one had visited the Priory when Jack heard stomping outside his door. The lock clicked free. The door swung open and after a lengthy pause, the giant monk lurched in with a tray in his hands and a bag slung over his shoulder. On the tray lay a bowl of hot fish stew and a loaf of bread for the dunking. Beside these tottered a pint-sized jug overflowing with foaming ale.

"Why did you lock me in?" Jack demanded, rushing across to confront him but halted by the aromas teasing his nostrils.

"As a precaution," the monk replied offhandedly as he placed the tray down on the table.

"Don't you trust me then?"

The monk glanced around the room and snorted at what he saw: the runnels of rain dribbling down from the furthermost wind-eye… the bed and two tables moved away from their proper positions… the bedsheet lying wet and crumpled on the floor.

"We are obliged to treat thee as our guest," he growled, "but that does not mean that we trust thee." He stared deeply into Jack's eyes, expressing unspoken contempt. "Especially since you've shown such an interest in our gold and silver."

Jack had to admit that this was not unreasonable. So ignoring the monk's hostility, he sat down on the bed and set about the food without further delay. The cleric unslung the bag, tugged out a pair of shoes, and dropped these unceremoniously on the floor. Then producing Jack's pouch and knife, he flung these onto the bed.

"From what you say," Jack said, unsheathing the dagger and using it to cut a slice off the loaf, "I'm surprised that you are allowing me to keep this."

The monk stared back with his eyebrows raised. "Why should we not?" he said. "One false move from you and you will be out of here quicker than a coney with a ferret on its tail."

Jack finished his food, licked the bowl quite clean and returned it to the tray. After draining the jug in one long swig, he lay back on the bed and belched loudly. The monk picked up the tray and stalked indignantly out. But instead of closing the door, he could be heard exchanging words with someone outside. Then the Scrivener scuttled in and flopped down on the bed.

"As if I haven't got enough to do," he muttered, fanning himself with a folded piece of parchment and thereby wafting across the stink of burnt feather, "I've had to come up here at the behest of an uncouth *strip*-ling like *you*."

Jack blanched. By putting the stress on '*strip*', the Scrivener revealed that he'd still found time to visit the Porter on the way up to see him. He glanced across at his candle. The pin had just fallen out and was rolling off the block.

"Are you wearing those three crosses to protect yourself from the Devil?" Jack asked, wishing that he possessed one for himself.

"One can't be too careful," the Scrivener said, producing an earthenware bottle from his satchel and placing it on the table. After tugging a quill from behind his ear, he used Jack's knife to shape and split its end. Aware of the door being quietly closed and locked, Jack dictated the petition as required by his former captors.

The Scrivener scribbled away with frequent bursts of sighing. "How many copies?" he asked when they had finished.

"Two please."

"That will be five silver pennies. Dostow have the money on thee?"

"I should have," Jack said, reaching for his pouch. "Yes, it's all here. Here you are." He counted out the coins. "One copy must be delivered to the Baron."

"He's away fighting the Scots," the Scrivener said as he packed his equipment away. "And in my experience, it will probably be mislaid by the time he gets back." He struggled ungainly to his feet. "He's left his Steward in charge. I suggest that you keep both copies and send the Steward a note to say that you have them."

"How much would that cost?"

"To write a short note... one penny. However, since we can't deliver it by hand, it will have to be flown up to the castle on one of their doves."

"How much?"

"Another penny."

That agreed, and the extra tuppence handed over, the Scrivener knocked loudly on the door and was quickly let out. And after hearing the lock refitted and footsteps dying away, Jack resumed his lonely vigil at the lancet.

***

Jack was nodding off to sleep when he was alerted by the clatter of hooves below his wind-eye. Taking the cover behind the edge of its embrasure, he peered down at the forecourt below. The rain had stopped, but the arch still looked flushed with anger at its prolonged soaking. Two black-cloaked riders sat facing the doors, their horses pawing constantly at the cobbles. The smaller rider sat sideways on a palfrey, her face completely hidden by her hood, and although the other's helmet hid his face, there was no mistaking that self-important manner. It was the Steward of Dudley Castle.

CHAPTER 13

The door was unlocked and the giant monk strode in.

"Somebody outside wants to see you," he said, grabbing Jack by the elbow.

Jack pulled back in sudden alarm. "Are you going to hand me over to the Steward?"

Instead of answering, the monk guided him firmly out through the open doorway. Hustled along the corridor, Jack consoled himself with the knowledge that the Prior had promised him sanctuary. He wouldn't go back on his word. Or would he? He'd also said that he couldn't upset the Baron.

Turning right at the bottom of the stairs, the monk hurried Jack towards the chapel door. As it was opened for him to enter, it scarcely registered that it was pointed at the top as he remembered. However, the Steward was not there – just the Porter and a gaggle of monks who were feigning disinterest. And the doors to the outside world were shut and bolted.

His panic over, Jack gradually recovered his senses. Once more the scent of incense filled the air. The angels on the walls resumed their glittering combat. The soothing sound of plainchant seeped softly through the rood screen. Nevertheless, it all seemed sinister now.

While making sure that the big doors were *really* bolted, he noticed the arch above them. It was half-round on the inside, while still pointed on the outside. Of course. He'd seen something similar at the castle – where different types of stonework recorded changes over the years. This chapel must be the same. And that was why the small door was confusing. *He wasn't losing his reason after all.*

Meanwhile, the Porter had opened a hatchway in the wall. Elbowing him aside, Jack peered into the speaking-tube thus revealed. Beyond it lay the fishpond, whose pockmarked surface confirmed that it was pittling down with rain. With incense fumes streaming past his nose, he whispered into the aperture:

"Is there anybody there?"

Immediately, a pair of angry eyes were staring back at him – quickly replaced by an angry be-whiskered mouth.

"WHO IS THAT?" There was no mistaking the Steward's accusing voice.

"It is I, Sire," Jack murmured hesitantly.

"Isaiah? Who the hell is that?"

Jack paused. Isaiah was the urchin who'd got him into this mess in the first place. "It's not Isaiah," he protested. "It's me."

"I know that voice." The whiskered mouth now twisted in contempt. "Is that you, soldier?"

Hearing himself thus addressed, Jack's spirits rallied slightly. Perhaps he wasn't beyond the pale yet after all.

"Y-yes, Sire," he said, unable to control the trembling in his voice. "I have c-claimed s-sanctuary here."

"So it *is* you," bellowed the Steward, squinting angrily up the hole. "You are in even *bigger* trouble now."

Jack had to think fast and he wasn't used to it.

"I c-can explain everything," he spluttered. "I was k-kidnapped by a band of k-knaves. They agreed to spare my life if I would get their p-petition writ and p-present it to the Baron."

"A *petition*?" The Steward almost choked on that insolent word. "They *dare* to present a petition to the *Baron*?" He gasped for breath. "Well they're out of luck. He's up there fighting the Scots. Anyway, what's it about?"

"It's about them needing food to feed their starving families."

"Why? We allow them to keep what they manage to grow for themselves."

"That was all eaten long ago." In desperation, Jack decided to try a different approach: that of asking for advice. "What should I do with their petition, Sire? I've just had it written and I have it here."

"I know what I'd *like* to do with it," the Steward growled. "Nevertheless, you'd better give it to me."

"Will you send it to the Baron, Sire?"

"No. I shall deal with it myself ... one way or another."

After retrieving it from his pouch, Jack pushed the folded parchment into the aperture, the wax seal scraping softly on damp cement. When the Steward couldn't quite reach it, Jack looked around for some way of shoving it further. Finding a fishing pole propped up nearby, he poked the precious document down the tunnel, ready to let go the rod should it be grabbed.

"So what's this all about?" the Steward muttered, to the sounds of the seal being snapped and the rustle of parchment being unfolded.

"That was meant for the Baron's eyes only," Jack protested, to the restless shuffle of shoes behind his back.

"As I just told you," the Steward growled impatiently, "the Baron is away supporting the King in the north of the country. The peasants have *me* to deal with now."

So Gran had been right about that. She was probably also right about the Steward not knowing how to deal with the peasants' demands.

"As you see, Sire," Jack said, throwing caution to the winds, "they're only seeking the Baron's help to feed their families through the famine." Taking a deep breath, he added: "They also say that what little grain they can find for sale costs far more than they can afford. So they are asking for the price to be brought back down to what it was last year. And ..."

"*AND?*" the Steward roared.

Jack faltered in his resolve. Should he go on or not? Plucking up his courage, he decided to continue. "It doesn't say so there, but ..." He began to gabble. "They say that ifallelse fails, they're *not*goingtoharvest thisyear's grainuntil they get his agreement."

There! He'd got the words out somehow, but at what cost to himself?

"Anything else?" the Steward demanded sarcastically.

"Yes!" (In for a penny, in for a groat.) "They want it all written down so as to be legally binding in the courts. Oh! And there are to be no reprisals." He'd said it *all* now. Or rather, he'd got rid of the treasonable words before he choked on them.

The face beyond the aperture had flushed almost as red as the arch outside.

"What you say does seem to be the sooth," the Steward muttered grimly. "*NEVERTHELESS*: once I get my hands on those knaves, it will all be legally binding all right. Legally binding around their insolent necks. And that of course, also applies to *you*."

"But I'm only the messenger," Jack screamed into the hole, ignoring the shushes of the monks now crowded round him.

"I demand to see the Prior," the Steward bawled. "The sooner I prise you out of there the better."

"But I've been granted sanctuary here," Jack cried, to more shushes.

"We'll see about *that*. Is there anybody in there with you?"

"Only the Porter and some monks."

"Let me speak to him."

"Who?"

"Who d'you think? The bloody Porter."

"He wants to speak to you," Jack said, turning to the doorkeeper at his elbow.

"Yes?" the monk enquired, staring calmly into the hole. "Can I be of help?"

Jack had to stand by and listen to one side of the conversation:

"Ye want what?... All right, you *demand* what?... To have this lad delivered up into your hands?" (Jack quailed.) "I'm afraid that it cannot happen until forty days and nights have passed. What?... You demand to see the Prior? I'm afraid you can't at the moment... Why? Because he's leading the prayers... You'll wait? Very well then, but he's a very busy prior. Wait there wilt thou?...What? You want... er, demand to come in out of the rain? Have you brought any soldiers with you?...No? On your word? Very well. I'll go and consult Prior Robert as soon as he's free... Oh! In about half an hour. You'll come

75

back with a warrant? We must insist that it is signed and sealed by the Baron... Well if that's what you think, I bid thee good day."

The Porter backed away from the hole and slammed its little hatch. "Take him back up to the dorter, wilt thou Brother?" he asked the giant monk.

In a state of hopeless despair, Jack allowed himself to be hustled back up the staircase to the guest dormitory. As he threw himself down on his bed, he heard the Steward complaining bitterly outside:

"How d'you like that? They say that a warrant will have to be signed and sealed by the Baron."

Jack crept across to the wind-eye. The Steward had remounted his horse and was wheeling it around to face his silent companion. "That will take weeks," he bawled as he rode off towards the causeway.

The female rider sat staring at the doors. Although her face was still covered by her hood, Jack shook with a lightning-flash of recognition.

Hearing his gasp above her, she threw back that hood and gazed up with eyes agleam with tears.

It was Felicia. But now so haggard as to seem no longer beautiful – even to Jack's besotted and lovelorn eyes. Nevertheless, his heart stopped beating, and in that timeless moment, an unspoken bond was forged between the two.

With one last lingering look, Felicia turned her horse about and rode off after her father. Soon they appeared on the farther shore and he watched until she'd ridden out of sight.

Some time later, Jack was awakened from his doze by the giant monk shaking his shoulder. "The Prior wants to see you," he announced. "Right now," he added as Jack rushed past him into the passageway.

Another trip round the cloisters ... another knock on the door, and the Prior was waving him in for the second time. Jack marched up to his table.

"Are you handing me over to the Steward after all? You said that I could stay here."

"And so thou shalt. I have sent him to get a warrant signed by the Baron; and even when he produces it I shall have to get permission from our priory at Wenlock, and the prior there will probably seek advice from Cluny."

"Where's Cloony?"

"In France."

"But they say that France and England are on the verge of war."

"Precisely."

For the first time in his life, Jack could see some benefit in having alien monasteries.

"In the meantime," the Prior said, proffering a seat, "I have been thinking about the peasants' situation."

Jack said nothing, more concerned with his own uncertain future.

"I have decided," the Prior continued, "that whether or not the Baron releases food from the castle, I shall send some out from here."

In spite of his anxiety, Jack grinned inwardly. His gran's plan seemed to be working after all.

"I must inform them about it without delay," the Prior added. "Havest thou any suggestions as to how this might be accomplished?"

"Send one of your monks out to tell 'em," Jack said vaguely.

Again that little smile. "That is *quite* out of the question. Everyone must stay within the confines of the Priory until the present danger has passed."

Now that Jack came to think of it, it was ages since he'd seen any monks abroad in the town.

"Nevertheless," the Prior insisted, "I must let the peasants know immediately."

"Some of them are out there surrounding your moat. I've tried to get 'em to come across and parley, but they don't seem to want to. If I had my bow and arrows, I could shoot a message to 'em across the lake."

"We have the Porter's bow," the priest said thoughtfully.

"I'd rather stay away from *him*, if you don't mind."

"Why is that?" the priest demanded, his eyebrows raised. "Did he not treat thee with sufficient courtesy?"

"A bit too much courtesy for my liking." Jack hadn't meant to say that, but it had slipped out all by itself.

"And what dost thou mean by that?"

Jack described the monk's close attention as he stripped himself stark naked.

"And thou thinkest that he was eyeing thee out of *lust*?"

Jack remained silent.

"Nay," the Prior said, smiling his little smile. "I admit that there are some here who find the celibate life… rather… difficult." He slapped the table with the flat of his hand. "But our Porter is most certainly not one of them. He was probably remembering the way he once used to be. He was Dudley's champion archer for a time."

Jack almost laughed out loud. The man didn't look the type.

"Oh yes. He didn't always have that paunch. When he first arrived here, he was as strong as an ox. Broad shoulders. Chest like a barrel. Muscular arms. Legs like tree trunks." He sighed. "He's not like that now, of course. But what's left of his strength comes in useful for opening those doors."

Jack expected the flicker of a smile, but it didn't reappear.

"Unfortunately," the Prior said, pursing his lips, "he accidentally shot an arrow-boy in the back."

Jack had heard of such an accident, but had never learned what happened after that.

"He came to us in penitence," the priest continued. "We still have his bow and arrows in our storeroom. I shall have them sent up to the guest room without delay. That reminds me…" The Prior was peering in a most peculiar manner. "The Porter used to wield a sword as well."

Jack said nothing. What was *that* to do with him?

"Yes," said the Prior quickly. "I've just had an idea. We might use your skill at arms to fight for us."

I suggested that to *you*, Jack thought. At least, I think it was me that thought of it. He was about to point this out when a voice inside his head urged caution. *Nay lad. 'Tis better if he thinks it's his own idea.*

"You could be very useful to us," the Prior continued, smiling broadly. "We have many disputes with our tenants over who has title to the lands they farm."

"Yes?" Jack said, pretending to be interested.

"Well, when the deeds can not be found, the only course left open is trial by combat."

"You want *me* to fight for your rights?"

"Yes. That's if the Baron can be persuaded, of course."

"But won't the Steward have something to say about that?"

"He can have his *say*, but…" the Prior placed two fingers alongside his nose, "…we shall have our *way*. We wield considerable power behind the scenes. Even the nobles are afraid of excommunication."

His fears in no way allayed, Jack shuffled in his chair. "From what you say, someone has been doing your fighting in the past."

"Oh yes! Our Porter did it for a while, but his heart wasn't really in it." He sighed. "In fact, he lost us so much property that we had to find a substitute. Then Brother Michael tried his hand. But in spite of his great strength and length of reach, his first and only bout was a complete disaster. I think that somebody must have been teaching the peasants new tricks." He peered intently into Jack's eyes. "It wasn't *you* was it?"

"No, it wasn't me," Jack said – having only just begun to do so. "But I'm willing to give it a go if the Baron agrees to let me." Not much chance of *that*, he thought. However, even the suggestion might buy him more time to plot his next moves.

"Very well. I shall get someone to sort out our manual of single combat for you to study."

"But I told you: I can't read."

"I have *not* forgotten that," the Prior said irritably. "The pictures are self-explanatory. You won't need to read the instructions right away. Actually…" The fleeting grin reappeared. "I have already appointed someone to teach you your letters. He's waiting up there in the dorter as we speak."

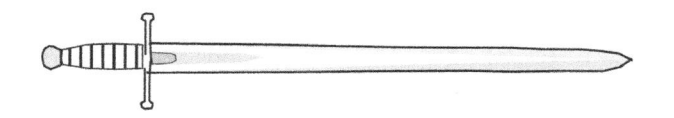

CHAPTER 14

"Hello," said a youth as Jack stepped into the dormitory. It was the one who'd taken the whipping in the cloister. "The Prior has ordered me to learn you how to read."

"Am I allowed to speak?" Jack whispered as the door was closed and locked behind him.

"Why yes. How else can we do it?" The youth held out his hand. "I'm Brother Cedric. What's your name?"

Jack told him, adding: "Why were you being whipped, back there in the cloister?"

"For forgetting the words of a prayer." Brother Cedric had answered lightly, but he was easing his habit away from his rounded buttocks. "I deserved it. It's an insult to Lord Jesus when I get it wrong."

Jack decided to voice no opinion about that. Nevertheless, it was a very strange 'house of God' that made lads suffer – even though that was what Jesus had chosen for himself. He walked to the lancet wind-eye and looked out. "Has anybody arrived here recently?"

"None that I know of."

"How can you be so cheerful?" Jack asked, seeing that the lad was smiling.

Cedric laughed. "Compared to the will of God, what else matters?" He produced some squares of parchment and spread them out like playing cards on the bed. "Come and take a look at these. I've written down some of the letters for you to learn."

Together, they examined the first of them.

"The easiest one is the Ess," said Cedric, "See? It looks like a snake and it sounds like one as well. Sssss. Why aren't you looking?"

"I'm worried about the Devil. What if he comes in here when I'm locked in on my own?"

"Why on Middle-Earth would you worry about *that*?"

Jack told him about the inkblot.

"Oh, take no notice of him," Cedric said, referring to the Scrivener. "He sees signs and portents everywhere. That must come from copying out all those old manuscripts." He slapped Jack on the back. "Don't worry. The Devil can't get at you here. There are prayers being said all the time." He laughed a self-diminishing little laugh. "In fact, there are so many of 'em that I keep getting the words mixed up."

"Hence your whipping?"

"Hence my whipping."

"But you don't understand," Jack moaned. "Somebody... or... some*thing*, keeps putting sinful thoughts into my head."

"I get that all the time," Cedric whispered from behind his hand.

"Really?"

"Oh yes." He stared vacantly into the distance. "Especially when young women come down to the lake to bathe."

"What do you do then?" Jack asked.

"What d'you think?" He chuckled conspiratorially. "I watch 'em. Then I go and tell my confessor."

"What happens then?"

"He absolves me on condition..."

"On condition of what?" said Jack. "That you take another whipping?"

"No," said Cedric, smirking. "On condition that I fetch him the next time they come." He grinned even more widely. "I've heard that he then confesses his sinful thoughts to the next priest up the line... and so on and so forth until it gets right up to the Prior." He chuckled again. "So you see, you've got nothing to worry about on that score. We men are all the same, and you don't grow out of it with age."

Jack sat down, blushing and bridling. "Are any of those women from the castle?"

"I don't think so. Judging by the shabby dresses that they come down in, they're just poor wenches from the town."

Jack fell silent, picturing Felicia at her bathing. He shook his head to dispel the agreeable image. "I'm having those thoughts right now," he wailed.

"That's nothing to get upset about."

"I can't help it. I've been admiring women for as long as I can remember."

"Me too."

"But the priest up at the castle says that it's all the work of the Devil."

"That can't be true. After all, since we are all originally created by God, why should He object if we admire His handiwork?"

As Jack paused to consider the implications of that, Cedric continued brightly: "As Saint Paul once said: It's better to wed than to burn."

"Does that mean: either get married or burn in Hell?"

"I don't know. From what I've seen of my parents' marriage, that *was* hell on earth. That's why I'm here," he added sadly.

Marriage. Jack had never thought of marriage. But now that he *had*, the idea of waking up next to Felicia filled his heart with a sudden longing.

"I can see that you're still worried," Cedric said as he unslung a cross from around his neck. "Wear this. I've got another one downstairs."

Hauled reluctantly back from his reverie, Jack accepted the cross and slid its thong over his head. Somewhat comforted by the protection, he picked up the 'Ess' card. "So what did you say this was?"

"That's the 'S.' It sounds and looks like a snake. Sssss."

Jack repeated the sound. "Sssss." He grinned. "That's easy enough. What next?"

"Not so fast. Follow the line with your finger as you say it: Ssssssss."

Jack did as he was told. "Sssssssss."

"That's it. Keep doing that while I rub some of your candle fat on me bum."

"I hope you don't think that I'm stupid," Jack said after he'd repeated the task for the umpteenth time, "but I can't really see much point in this."

"Keep at it, Brother. We all have to start somewhere. The thing about the 'S' is that it's written the same whether it's a capital letter or a little one."

This meant nothing to Jack, but he didn't care to admit it.

"Stop looking at me like that," Cedric muttered, moving further away. "Try and concentrate on what I'm showing you. You don't want to end up with a backside like mine, do you?"

"I'd like to see 'em try," Jack whispered to himself.

The next letter to be learned was capital 'T'. Shaped like a gibbet made for two, its sound was a tutting noise. They had just got to the letter 'P' when the giant monk came shuffling in through the doorway. He'd brought the Porter's bow (its string hanging loose against the stave), one sharp-tipped arrow, one spare string and a narrow strip of parchment covered with writing.

"The Prior sent you these," he muttered, tossing them onto the letter-cards.

"What does this say?" Jack asked, seizing the Prior's parchment and staring at it blankly.

"Give it here and I'll show you," Cedric replied as he reached for the arrow.

Jack watched as the youth read out the message – spelling out each word and tracing the individual letters with the point of the arrow. It was an offer of a regular supply of 'Hweat and Baerley' for as long as the famine continued. Jack grinned as he saw how each group of letters represented a single word – and how the first letter of 'Baerley' looked a bit like a pair of Breasts.

In the meantime, the giant monk had been trying to string the bow.

"Not like that," Jack shouted, leaping up and grabbing it. "Here, I'll show you how it should be done."

Ignoring the monk's resentment, Jack rested the bow's lower nock against the side of his left shoe. Grasping the handgrip with his left hand, he pressed his right hand's palm against the upper limb of the bow. His thumb and finger held the bowstring taut, ready to slide its loop up into the top nock. But despite all his pulling and pushing, he could not get it anywhere near the groove. He now regarded the weapon with great respect. This six-foot stave of straight-grained yew had a handgrip too thick to encompass with his fingers. "It will take a mightier man than me to draw this bow," he admitted shamefacedly. "No wonder the Porter was so successful at the butts."

"I suppose I should try and help you," the giant monk muttered, "since the Prior is so insistent." Moving quickly to Jack's rear (much to his discomfort) he moved up close with his mouth against his ear. "Try it again and I'll give you a helping hand. Two hands, in fact." So as Jack repeated his attempt at stringing the bow, the monk enclosed his hands within his own great fists. And as they pulled and pushed the stave together, the string's loop slid up into the waiting groove.

After fitting the arrow onto the string, Jack flexed the bow a little – both gauging its feel and awakening its dormant sinews.

The giant monk backed away, his hands upraised.

"There's no need to fear me," Jack laughed. "I cannot draw this bow enough to hurt thee." This was not really true. He could only haul the arrow back by half its length, but there was still enough power in the bow to kill – although not sufficient to shoot across the lake. "That's it then," he announced, propping the bow against the wall, whereupon its string hummed in derision for a while. "We can't deliver the Prior's message after all."

Cedric tiptoed to the door, looked out and scuttled back. "Why is it so urgent?"

Jack flopped down on the bed. "The peasants are now so desperate that they're planning to seize some food by force of arms." With his audience glancing at one another in fear and apprehension, he continued hurriedly. "They thought of attacking the castle but it's much too well-defended. This priory is their second choice." He picked up the Prior's parchment. "This is an attempt at buying them off by sending out food."

The giant monk moved to the nearest of the tiny wind-eyes and opened up its shutter.

"Perhaps it's just as well that we *can't* shoot out through here," he muttered while peering across the lake. "If the men over there are getting ready to attack, an arrow from us could have given them some justification."

"*Those* men aren't thinking of attacking you," Jack said quickly. "They're only here to get their petition written."

"What petition?" the monks enquired in unison.

Jack sighed. "Before their hot-heads get completely out of hand, the older peasants decided to petition the Baron – begging him to release some food from the castle's storehouse."

"Does the Prior know about this?"

"Yes. I told him as soon as I got here."

"*Typical*," the giant monk grumbled, still staring across the lake. "He never tells us *anything*. We have to rely on what the lookouts bother to mention." Breathing a sigh of either relief or regret, he turned back into the room. "They reported seeing a troop of men marching into the lychgate. Not long after that, *you* arrived on the pretext of claiming sanctuary. Then they saw a lant-horn flash, and *you* have obviously been using that bedsheet to signal out of that other wind-eye." Seeing Jack's discomfort, he added: "Remind me to get it washed and dried wiltow? Now where was I? Ah yes. Taking these things into account, we concluded that they were Barnsdale men, come to steal our gold, and that you had claimed asylum just to let the b… robbers in."

"I am *not* a spy," Jack protested hotly. "And those men are only there to make sure that I don't escape."

"So they'll leave us alone as soon as they get their petition writ? Is that what you are saying?"

"Well, after I've delivered it to the Baron." Jack tried to force a smile, but his mouth wouldn't let him. "I've done that already. Actually, I had to give it to his Steward instead. And I've asked for asylum to keep out of his and those knaves' clutches."

"But if their petition has already been presented," the giant monk said quietly, "why is our Prior offering to send them food as well?" He paused, the light of realisation in his eyes. "Of course: to dispel their antagonism towards us. That's good enough for me." Retrieving the bow, he handed it back to Jack. "And I'm going to help you to do it."

"How can you do that?" Jack asked, surprised.

"You'll see," the monk replied, and turning back to Cedric added: "Bind the Prior's message to the arrow wiltow? Just behind the head."

"What with, Brother Michael?"

"Cut a bit off that spare bowstring."

When the youth had obeyed his order, Brother Michael took the missile from him and handed it to Jack. "Where's the best place to drop it?" he asked.

"I'll show you from down there," Jack said, pointing to the furthermost end of the room. "By the way," he added as they walked between the opposing rows of beds, "the Prior is thinking of enlisting me as his champion."

The giant monk gave Jack a sideways glance. "Rather you than me," he said with obvious sympathy.

"Why do you say that?"

"What? Given the choice of either hacking some poor sod-tiller to death or becoming a martyr to the Prior's endless greed? No, thank you very much." He paused, seeing that Cedric was hanging on every word. "Not a word of this to anyone if you please."

"You know me better than that."

"So, how did you manage to get out of it?" Jack asked.

"I'll tell you later. When this task is done."

Jack reopened the shutter of the furthest little wind-eye. Beyond it lay a stretch of sparkling water, for the rain had stopped and the sun was shining brightly. The wind had dropped to aid them in their task.

"The lychgate's round to the right," he said, "so we cannot hit it from here. We'll just have to drop the arrow on the footpath."

Brother Michael yawned and stretched out his arms. "Well, we'd better not kill anybody or the Prior will excommunicate us."

"He'd do *that*?" Jack cried, appalled. "He'd have us banned from Heaven when we die?"

"Not really," Cedric interposed. "But he'd make us do lots of penances to get our excommunications lifted."

"That is true," Brother Michael agreed. "The Archbishop of Canterbury excommunicated *him* once – although he got the Bishop of Worcester to annul it. But enough of that. Let's send the message."

It was going to be a restricted shot – what with the smallness of the wind-eye, the great thickness of the wall, and the thatch being so close above their heads. The great power of the bow would be a boon; if only Jack could draw it, the arrow would clear the lake without aiming high. Jack nocked the arrow to the string and drew it back as far as he was able – which was nowhere near enough to cover the distance.

"Hang on," said Brother Michael, moving up close again. His right hand gripped the bow above Jack's left, while his left hand's fingers hooked the string in likewise manner. Then, huddled cheek by shoulder, they hauled until the fletchings brushed Jack's chin – his chest not being appropriate for a low shot such as this.

"You release first," Jack said, his arms already shaking with the strain.

"After three then," the monk muttered grimly. "I shall count in Latin so that you can learn the numbers ... Oo-nus, Doo-oh, *Trrrayss*."

The string tore free from Jack's trembling fingers, driving the arrow out through the tiny wind-eye. Two straw-covered heads crammed into the narrow opening, watching the missile as it sped across the lake. Although viewed along its line of flight, Jack had never seen one going so fast before. Skimming the bushes on the opposite shore, it swooped like a sparrowhawk down towards *the Bailiff*. He was prowling along the shoreline and staring down at the path, which undoubtedly recorded the prints of the knaves' procession.

Unaware of his great danger, he stooped to pick up something from the ground. As he straightened up and carried on walking, the arrow pierced the spot that he'd just vacated. He hadn't seen it coming but he must have heard it land, for he turned and looked in vain for the source of the sound. The low angle of the arrow's arrival must have driven it shallowly through the mud. If the fletchings were all covered, the message might never be found. But at least one feather was showing; for the Bailiff marched to the spot where the arrow had vanished. Squatting down, he tugged on the shaft, trying to withdraw it from the ground intact. Finding this to be impossible, he snapped off the feathered end and wiped it on the grass. Together with the mud, the parchment slid off too, having been driven back against the flights by the force of the impact. After severing Cedric's binding, the Bailiff unrolled the sodden document and scanned the Prior's message with obvious displeasure. Then, thrusting it into his pouch, he squinted across at the Priory, whose shuttered wind-eyes stared back with blank disdain.

But one of those shutters wasn't quite closed. With his eye against the gap that he'd left for the purpose, Jack watched the Bailiff march off towards the castle.

"That's it then," he declared as he closed the shutter properly. "He didn't see the arrow land." Crossing his fingers behind his back, he added: "He's gone away now, so the knaves should find it soon. There's nothing else for us to do but wait."

"That's just as well," Cedric announced as the tower bell began to toll. "It's time for prayers."

CHAPTER 15

Jack lay back on his bed, a smile of nervous relief spreading over his features. The service in the chapel hadn't been as irksome as he'd feared. By watching Cedric's lips, he'd managed to mime the words, even though they made no sense at all to him.

Footfalls came a-clomping towards his door. Once more he heard the scrape and click as the lock released the hasp. As the door creaked open, Brother Michael called for Jack to get up and follow him.

*

The door to the chapel swung open, and the Porter stood framed in the entrance. "The Steward's back," he announced with a meaningful look.

"Has he come to arrest me?" Jack asked, pushing past the monk to scrutinise the great oak doors. Fortunately, they were shut and the bolts were still in place.

"Not that I know of," the Porter said, tugging on Jack's sleeve. "But before you speak to that bully out there, canstow tell me how our archers have been doing at the butts?"

Jack stepped back, amazed by the trifling question. Nevertheless, he forced himself to remember the last contest. "We lost," he said simply.

"Who to?"

"Who d'you think? Barnsdale Rovers."

"What was the final score?"

"Fifty golds to nil. Our blokes were so weak from hunger that they couldn't even reach the targets in the finals."

"Typical."

"Are you the one they call 'Strongbow'?" Jack asked, remembering a name that he'd heard somebody mention.

The monk blushed. "Probably not. That's the nickname of one of the nobs from long ago." He nodded towards the hatchway. "There's one of their lackeys out there now. You'd better find out what he wants."

The Steward's angry visage blocked the outer end of the speaking tube once more. It looked slightly less flushed than before.

"I've been thinking about your insolent petition," his voice thundered up the tiny passage, "and decided that... *that* it would be a..." (a gasp for breath) "...a *good* Christian act to provide the peasants with food from the castle storehouse." He paused for breath again. "However, you can tell your new masters that the price of grain is completely beyond my control."

"They are no masters of mine," Jack protested. "And now that I've been granted sanctuary here, they can't tell me what to do any more. But they *are* holding my grandmother hostage to make sure of my cooperation."

Silence fell – to the delight of the nearby monkitude.

"Very well!" the Steward said eventually. "I shall instruct the Bailiff to inform them that I agree to their dema... requests. *And* that I have given my word that there will be no reprisals – but *only* if they deliver the baxter into my hands unharmed." The Steward licked his lips, presumably in anticipation of her delicious crustades.

"But what about *me*?" Jack cried, fearing the probable answer. "Are you going to arrest me after all?"

"No," the Steward snapped. "It'll take too long to obtain the warrant." He coughed. "Your fellow conspirators have dem... have asked that your punishment be set aside. Well, so be it! But in its stead, you will be sent to join the Baron's contingent up in Newcastle. There will be no further punishments for you provided that you stay away from this manor."

"But the Prior has said that I could become a monk. Then I can stay here for good."

"You can forget about that!" the Steward rasped. "I have the Baron's permission to deal with the situation as I think fit. And I think fit to banish you from his lands."

"You mean for the rest of my *life*?" Jack wailed.

"Got it in one!" cried the Steward, turning to go. "And I warn thee not to try my patience any further, lest I change my mind."

Jack returned to the dormitory a state of mental turmoil. This was terrible. He'd been hoping to see Felicia from time to time. But once he was banished, he would never see her again.

That night, Jack was woken by something tinkling outside his wind-eye. Still in his monkish robe, he scrambled out of bed and peered around the shutter. Two white-enshrouded figures were waiting on the forecourt. One was at the speaking tube, apparently in conversation with the Porter. The other stood immediately below his wind-eye. A lant-horn dangled from one withered paw. The other clutched the bell.

Lepers. Swathed from head to foot in swaddling bands. He'd heard of extreme cases of disfigurement, but had never come across one before (thank the Lord). Now here were *two* such cases, arriving at night to hide their ugliness from prying eyes – eyes as unsympathetic as his own.

As if it had picked up his uncharitable thought, the nearest leper looked up sharply. After raising the lant-horn level with its face, it began to peel away a bloodstained bandage. Jack shrank back, fearful of what was going to be revealed. But curiosity prevailed. He'd never seen a leper's face before, and might not ever get the chance again. Gritting his teeth, he forced himself back to the wind-eye.

The bandage had fallen away. In the flickering light of the candle, the face upturned towards him was hideous in the extreme. Swellings and blisters erupted glistening fluids; yet there could be no mistaking that ghastly face, or the hair adhering to that scabby forehead, or the way that the head was tilted so fetchingly to one side. It was *Felicia*. It really *was* his darling.

He shrank away from the wind-eye, his heartbeat racing furiously; his hopes all dashed forever. *Nobody had told him that she'd got*

LEPROSY. That couldn't be right. Even if she *had* caught that terrible disease, how could it have got so advanced since last he'd seen her? Dreading more horrible disclosures, he looked out through the wind-eye again.

Felicia had scraped off one of her boils. The skin exposed was as fresh and smooth as ever. After rewinding the disgusting bandage, she pointed across the lake. She then tugged on the sleeve of her companion, who hurriedly pulled a bundle from the hatch. Together they sped along the bottom of the wall and vanished round the corner.

Jack gathered up the bedsheets and knotted them all together to form a rope. After tying one end to a bedpost, he clambered over the sill, squeezed through the narrow opening and lowered himself awkwardly to the ground. With his back pressed against the wall to avoid the speaking tube's line of sight, he sidestepped to the corner and away.

*

With the Priory left far behind, Jack heard an owl's hoot in the bushes straight ahead. Soon he was among those bushes. Felicia's arms were around his neck, and her body pressed so delightfully against his own. The scent of her filled his nostrils as, casting aside a revolting bandage, she kissed him on the lips. Oblivious now to the flour-paste excrescences, he gloried in the wonder of her closeness, certain now that he'd taken the right course of action. And although they had made themselves homeless, wherever the two of them might end up, *that* would be his home from now on. His heart was bound to Felicia's as surely as his feet had been bound together in the stocks. Whistling Felicia's accomplice out from her discreet hiding place, they set off hopefully in the direction of the Old Park.

Part Three

The
Citadel of the Giants

CHAPTER 16

Somewhere in the depths of the Baron's deer-park, Jack emerged from the shadows of the forest trees. Before him, a clearing lay bathed in the cool bright light of the rising moon. Every detail of the cottage was clearly visible: the unkempt thatch of its roof; the uneven plastering on its walls; the shuttered-up wind-eye. And all around, the trees stood silent and unmoving: a monochromatic mosaic of silver and black. As far as he could tell, there was nobody else about – except for Felicia and her maidservant who remained hidden at the dark woodland's edge. He still couldn't believe that the Steward's daughter had left her privileged life at the castle. Even more incredibly, she'd chosen to take her chances with a disgraced trainee soldier like himself.

Vigilant for any sign of danger, he crept across the unnervingly open expanse of soggy turf. The wicket gate creaked as he swung it open. Damn! He had forgotten about that. A dog barked. In an instant Jack was at its side, fondling its floppy ears and murmuring soothing words. The hound's throat rumbled with a growl that threatened to erupt into a second bark.

"It's all right Butch," Jack whispered. "Ye know me, surely?" By way of confirmation, the dog grinned widely and gave his hand a sloppy lick.

Still the cottage remained silent. Jack intensified his stroking and waved Felicia over to join him at the door.

*

Inside the cottage, Will Hawkes (Jack's friend and mentor, whom he still thought of as 'The Forester') was scrambling out of bed. He'd always relied on Butch to warn him of intruders. Not bothering to dress or find his slippers, he moved stealthily across to the shutter that covered the wind-eye. While peering through its spyhole, he unhooked his loaded crossbow from the wall.

The yard outside was just as he'd left it that evening. Butch was silent now, bless him! He'd recently taken to barking in his sleep. The Forester grinned. His old friend must have been reliving some incident of the chase.

No sound disturbed the silence. The chickens were all silent in their pens; no fox had crept up to intrude on their peaceful slumbers. Reassured and yearning for his bed, he shifted his head from side to side behind the loophole, scanning the familiar scene for one last time. Still nothing had changed. But wait: over to the right, a figure had appeared at the dark wood's edge. Clad from head to foot in snow-white bandages, its hood was tilted forward, its face concealed in shadow. If that was supposed to be a leper, it was not like any that he'd ever seen before. Lepers carried begging-bowls and bells, and that had neither. Here was no timid sufferer of that hateful and wasting disease. *This* figure stood proud, erect and motionless.

The leper's garb was a disguise. But why? There could be any number of reasons. The country was in turmoil. The King was at war with the Scots. The Welsh were threatening revolt, and the Earl of Lancaster was fomenting civil war. As usual, the barons were seizing the opportunity to take the law into their own hands... and throttle it to death! Amidst all this confusion, outlaws were wreaking havoc throughout the land, many having fallen foul of a law-system that had failed to protect them. Although the Forester had some sympathy for them, he never allowed *any* to trespass in 'his' woods. He couldn't risk antagonising the Baron yet again. Come daybreak, he'd gather a posse together and send the intruder packing.

As Will Hawkes stood debating with himself in the silent darkness, the figure began to move. Gliding silently across the silvered glade, it passed unhindered through the wicket gate that he'd carefully closed and bolted before turning in. To his even-great surprise, the figure did not turn towards the sheds that housed his livestock. Instead, it headed straight for the cottage door, possibly with murderous intent. During his years as a warrior and forester, Will Hawkes had made enemies…

Quickly raising the crossbow, he rammed its nose into the spyhole. With the front end thus supported by the shutter, he gripped and braced the stock against his shoulder. He took careful aim, sighting along his thumb to the killing-pile on the bolt. The releasing rod to send it on its way rested coldly on the fingers of his right hand. As the figure headed purposefully towards his door, he followed it with the bow. His fingers caressed the releasing-rod, easing it gently upwards and…

"Damn!" The right limb of the bow had jammed against the shutter, preventing him from keeping the figure in his sights. Then it was gone and he had missed his chance. It would be standing outside the door now. He waited for the sound of splintering wood, but all that he could hear was the pulsing of his heartbeat in his ears. Cold sweat broke out on his forehead. The figure had passed close enough to see its face, but *it didn't appear to have one.*

So it wasn't a robber after all, but a phantom. Had the Baron's dead brother escaped from his tomb to come in search of vengeance?

Thirteen years ago (possibly to the day) the assassin's arrow had struck Lord Roger down. They'd been thirteen long years of being haunted by his failure as custodian of the hunt. And during all those guilt-ridden years, he'd been paying the monks at the Priory to pray for Roger's soul. He'd also been making a donation for his *own* spiritual welfare, in the hope that the monks could reduce his time in Purgatory when his own end came. But the monks had grown greedier with each passing year, until their charges had become so excessive that he could no longer afford the payments.

It couldn't be a coincidence. Lord Roger's ghost had come to claim its dues in person. Well if that was the case: SO BE IT. Many times, had he seen his comrades killed in battle. Now it was *his* time to face his Nemesis like a man. Breathing deeply to stiffen his resolve, he marched to the door, unbarred and flung it open.

*

As Felicia approached the cottage, Jack was stooping to comfort the hound. The swinging door caught him fully on the crown.

*

A high-pitched shriek rent the silence as the Forester stepped forth to meet his doom. A fearful sight met his eyes. The apparition stood before him, moonlight reflected by the wall shining into its hood. But there were no features there; just a pair of glimmering eyes, staring back from a mess of putrefying flesh. The Forester stood frozen with horror as Jack, overcome with fury and resentment, threw his weight savagely against the door. It slammed into Will Hawkes' face, felling him as neatly as if he'd been poleaxed.

When the Forester regained consciousness, it was to find himself lying on his back with Butch licking furiously on his ear. So he hadn't been blasted into eternity after all. With amazed and watering eyes, he stared aghast at the doorway.

"Lord help me," he cried aloud. "Now I'm seeing double." There were *two* enshrouded figures there; one on either side of the open door.

"Nay, Forester." The voice at his other ear was that of the youth who'd once saved his life.

"Jack? What the hell are *you* doing here?" He'd whispered it without daring to move his head.

"I've brought my Lady Felicia and her servant," Jack's voice announced. "We're here seeking your assistance."

Ignoring his bleeding nose and aching forehead, the Forester gazed doubtfully at the spectral pair. Felicia was name of the Steward's daughter – although by all accounts, she was no lady. And though she wasn't what you would call *pretty*, she was a damn sight better-looking than either of the white-swathed figures who stood facing him now. Still hovering in the doorway, their faces glimmered blankly in the light of a newly lit candle.

"If those *are* real women," the Forester muttered, sitting up and holding his throbbing head, "they're the ugliest women that I have ever laid eyes on. How d'you expect *me* to help 'em? I am no magician. Anyway, why have you come calling on me at this ungodly hour?"

"We've run away from the castle," Jack said simply.

"*Hell's teeth*! Why would you do THAT? You know that you cannot survive without your lord and family."

"We had no choice," Jack protested. "I was accused of stealing some tarts to give to my kinfolk, and then I had to endure being locked in the stocks with my silly old grandmother, and then we were kidnapped, and then I escaped from the Priory and then—"

"Stop!" cried the Forester, struggling to his feet. "Start again, but slowly. Tell it as it happened, lad. You say that you were caught stealing from the castle?"

Indignant at having to go over it all again, Jack related how an act of misplaced generosity had got him involved with a gang of local knaves. And how by gaining sanctuary in the Priory, he had presented their petition to the Steward. Then he'd fled from there with Felicia and her maidservant Marion, both of whom were standing before him now.

All this time, the shrouded pair stood silent and unmoving. But now that the formal introductions had been made, the taller of the figures produced a polished steel mirror and began to peel away her face. The Forester watched amazed as the features of the Steward's daughter were slowly revealed to view. With her face besmirched with powdery flakes, she looked even less attractive than he remembered. What on earth did Jack see in her? Her figure? As if she'd read his thoughts, she began to unwind strips of cloth from round her body. And when she'd finished, he had to admit that it *was* worth looking at. Beneath the leper's shroud, she'd been wearing a figure-hugging gown of scarlet velvet, tailored to show her shapeliness to perfection. The sweet scent of roses overcame the lingering smell of coney-broth, but then recoiled defeated.

The second spectre now began to scrape the mess from off its face. But even when still besmirched with flour-paste pustules, Marion's face was far more attractive than her mistress's – oval in shape, with dark lustrous eyes, pert nose and a sensuously pouting mouth. Both men stared entranced as the last traces of flour were gently wiped away.

"Why haven't I seen you at the castle?" Jack asked in wonder.

"Because," exclaimed Felicia, stepping smartly in front of her servant, "Marion has only just arrived there." She linked her arm possessively into Jack's. "That's enough about *her*. What my Jack hasn't yet told you is that you were both to be sent to the front line in the Scottish wars. Not only that, I overheard my father ordering one of his men to deploy you in the fiercest part of the fighting." She lowered her voice to a whisper. "If the Scots didn't kill you, English arrows were to do it instead. Neither you nor my Jack would return to Dudley alive."

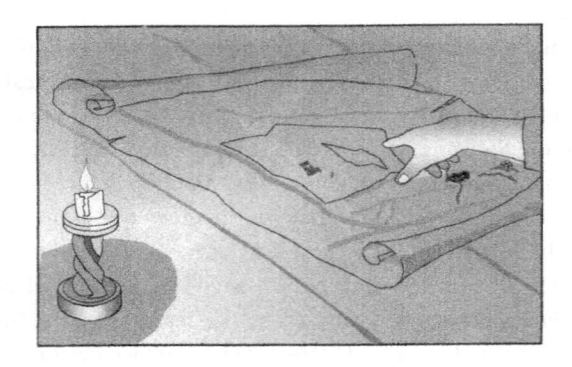

CHAPTER 17

The Forester's dark little cottage had fallen silent. Well, almost silent. There were the soft padding sounds of him pacing the earthen floor, and the even softer slurpings as his visitors spooned up soup from his sycamore bowls.

Jack and his beloved were sitting side by side at his rough-hewn table. Jack couldn't have told you what he was eating. With the thigh of his beloved pressing hard against his own, he could feel the warmth and firmness of her flesh. Felicia, however, was finding the situation difficult. Finally, she spat a spoonful out.

"This is tasteless muck," she announced, her mouth twisting with disgust. "He's forgotten the salt and pepper."

Her host stopped in his tracks.

"I am very sorry, my *Laydee*. But I can't afford the luxuries you've enjoyed at the castle. Nevertheless, that is good wholesome food."

"Please partake of another portion, my precious," Jack coaxed. By adopting what he thought to be a gentlemanly mode of speech, he'd spat a sprinkling of breadcrumbs over her face. "After all," he added, "who knows when we'll be able to eat again."

"Thank you very much," Felicia muttered, wiping her face with a discarded strip of bandage.

"What for?"

"Oh! Shut up and eat your gruel."

Leaning forward to rest both fists on the table, the Forester glowered down at his uninvited guests. "So where are you planning on going to next?" As Felicia forced more of his precious liquid past her increasingly unwilling lips, he waited impatiently for an answer. "Did anyone see you leave the castle?" he demanded finally.

Seeing that her mistress was finding it hard to swallow both his food and his insolent manner, Marion coughed at the other end of the table. Still wrapped in its cheesecloth covering, her arm waved, wraithlike, at the limit of the candlelight.

"Nobody saw us go," she said in the ensuing silence. "We're sure of that. My mistress had obtained a key to the postern gate. And I had – er – enticed the guard to be guarding somewhere else."

The Forester gave her a long hard look and then resumed his pacing.

"Well you can't stay here," he said, giving Jack an apologetic glance as he stalked past. "The Steward will come here first when he finds you gone."

"Why is that?" Felicia asked.

"Because," Jack said, putting an arm protectively around her shoulders and hugging her close, "this man and me once fought off a band of men who were trying to kill us."

"Is that when you hacked somebody's arm off?" she asked while looking from one to the other.

Before Jack could think of a suitable answer, the Forester was pacing the floor again.

"I know that the Baron still blames me for his brother's death," he muttered morosely, "but I never thought that he would send me off to mine. And I was thinking myself highly valued as the protector of his deer." He stopped and stared questioningly at Jack. "But why should he want to get rid of *you*? If it hadn't been for you, he wouldn't have been able to prove that the Wyntertons killed his brother."

"That wasn't the *Baron's* idea," Felicia cried, clutching at Jack's free hand. "Jack's only fault is that he dared to woo me … if only with his eyes." She gazed adoringly up at the young man at her side. "With those long lashes and dark brown eyes, he won my heart completely. It's my *FATHER*, the Steward, who wants him killed."

Jack kissed her on the cheek and hugged her even harder.

The Forester seemed embarrassed. "So you couldn't prevail on him to accept your choice of husband?" It was a statement of obvious fact, rather than a question.

"*Nay,*" cried Felicia bitterly. "Jack is of such common stock."

Jack blushed. It was true. Nobody's stock was any commoner than his. Moreover, his initial feelings of wonder and joy at the girl's affection had become largely overshadowed by the fear of what would happen if her father caught up with them.

Felicia now related how she'd pleaded on Jack's behalf, thus preventing him from being sent to the quarries '*for the rest of his miserable life*'.

"So *where* are you going to now?" the Forester asked again.

"I have relatives in Shropshire," Felicia snapped. "We can stay with them until we find somewhere more permanent. And I have kinfolk in France that we might—"

"As for tonight, Jack interrupted, "we are heading for Brewood Priory. We were hoping that you would guide us for part of the way."

"Why go there?"

"If the peasants' petition had failed," Jack said, "they were going to join the outlaws up in Barnsdale. The Priory is on the way there, and the Prioress of the Black Nuns has offered them her protection." (Felicia flinched on receiving another shower of spittle and crumbs.) "We are hoping that she'll do the same for us."

"The Prioress is in no position to offer shelter to *anyone,*" the Forester announced quietly. "She's been arrested for petty larceny."

"Oh no!" Felicia moaned. "We were hoping that she'd marry us whilst we were there. After all, my father would hardly have his *son-in-law* killed... would he?"

Because Jack hadn't any sisters, he regarded all good-looking women with awe and wonder. The fact that Felicia should even think of marrying him was scarcely believable. Nevertheless, things were happening much too quickly for his liking. Of the Steward's subsequent change of attitude towards him, he was not optimistic.

The Forester strode to the door and swung it shut.

"You realise that in order to get to Shropshire," he said while slotting the beam across to make it secure, "you'll have to cross Wynterton's lands." When Felicia shrugged her shoulders, he ignited a second candle from the first and set them both down on the table. "And remember," he added, "they would give a fortune to lay their hands on the Steward's daughter."

"That's why we've come to you for help," Felicia murmured, folding her arms protectively over her chest.

The Forester laughed mirthlessly. "And here was I, thinking that you'd come to warn me of my danger."

"That too, of course," said Felicia hurriedly. "Our interests lie together in this, I think."

The Forester made no reply. Felicia's use of the word 'lie' had alerted him to the fact that she might not be telling the truth. Or at least not the whole of it.

"Well whatever you decide to do," he snapped, "you'll have to be quick about it."

Picking up one of the candlesticks, he marched across to an iron-bound chest in the corner. He returned with a roll of parchment. After sweeping the table free of crumbs and mouse-droppings with the back of his hand, he unrolled the scroll upon the soup-smeared surface. Finding the light of two candles inadequate for making out the details, he returned to the chest and brought back several more. He lit these in quick succession, then nodded at the spyhole in the shutter.

"Stuff something into that, wiltow Jack. We don't want to attract attention."

Once he'd blocked the hole with a wad of discarded bandage, Jack rejoined the others at the table. To the crackling and sputtering of the candles, they studied what was now revealed to be a map. The most obvious feature was a wavy green line which surrounded a roughly square area. "That represents this park," the Forester said. Sure enough, three words had been written inside it. The first began with a '**T**', followed by two letters that Jack didn't recognise. The second had three that he'd never seen before. The third was a '**P**', followed by three more unknown characters. Together, they must spell '**THE OLD PARK**'. To prove the point, the wavy green line had a sketch of the Priory outside its lower right-hand corner. At some distance above its upper boundary, a smudge had the letters: '???**PT**??' scribbled beside it. That must be '**HAMPTON**' town.

His delight at making these deductions gave way to depression. How could he hope to take care of his beloved? Apart from a few local places, he didn't know where anywhere was. And he could hardly read the writing on a map. Thank goodness he'd got the Forester to rely on.

"Brewood is right up here." The Forester had pushed the scroll further open and was pointing at a spot near its upper left-hand corner. Compared with the size of the park, it looked a very long way away. "And the lands between there and Hampton..." the finger slid down towards that town's smudge, "are controlled by the Bushburys. And here ..." the finger moved to the right across the parchment, "the Swynnertons. Not very long ago, they were all Lancaster's men. They even killed Robert de Essington when he tried to collect taxes for the King. And what do you think happened when they were arrested and prosecuted?" He surveyed his silent audience. "They pretended to be priests. And when that didn't work, they paid a jury to swear on oath that they were innocent." He sighed with exasperated fury. "Not long after that, they transferred their allegiance to the King and he pardoned them for their crimes. But it hasn't stopped them attacking one another – or the Baron of Dudley for that matter. What I'm telling you is: *they are all your enemies.*"

"What about going south, then?" Jack asked. "You once told me that Hales is in part of Shropshire. Could we claim sanctuary there?"

"You might," admitted the Forester, but immediately shook his head in refutation. "No you can't!" he announced. "The white monks of the abbey rely on the Baron for their protection. And remember, his mother lives in Weoley Castle not far away. Not only that, the De Somerys have lands between there and London. No! South is out."

"Hurry up and decide what we should do," cried Felicia. "We haven't got all night."

"I know that as well as you do!" said the Forester angrily. "But these are uncertain times. Would estow risk straying into enemy lands?"

"Don't fall out," Jack cried, grabbing both their hands. "You are both too precious to me."

Felicia dodged more flying breadcrumbs. "Very well my dearest," she said, smiling sweetly at the Forester. "How many horses have you got?" she demanded of him.

"Only one," he snapped back at her, "and she's not bred for speed, but for skulking about in the woods."

"Why not head west for Wales?" Marion murmured from the shadows.

"Oh yes!" snorted Felicia. "And the Welsh will welcome us with open arms will they? I don't think so. Not after what Longshanks has been doing to them."

"They might do," Marion countered quietly. "They are always attacking the King's allies in the Marches. We could offer to help them to capture Dudley Castle. They would surely reward us well if they gained control of the English heartlands."

"We cannot do *that*," Felicia cried. "My father is the Steward."

"But you said that you wanted to get back at him," her servant reminded her.

"Not *that way*."

"We have friends up there in the castle," the Forester added. "What a stupid idea."

"Pardon me for speaking," Marion mumbled from somewhere else in the darkness.

"Well what ARE we going to do then?" Felicia cried. "If we cannot go north, south or... *what are you two gawping at*?" Both men were gazing at something behind her back. Freeing herself from Jack's embrace, she swivelled around on her stool. "Oh I seeeeee!"

Jack's plug of rag had fallen from the shutter's spyhole. Silhouetted against the moonbeam that came streaming in, Marion was removing the first of her leper's bandages. As she twisted around, her form could be clearly seen through its cheesecloth covering. And she *wasn't wearing anything underneath*. Both men stared entranced as the strip drifted down to the floor. Unaware of the attention, she twisted round to grope for the end of another.

Two sharp intakes of breath were followed by exhaled exclamations: "*Wow me!*", that age-old expression of men's admiration of women.

"Why not go east, then?" Marion murmured as she cast the second strip away with graceful abandon.

"What?" spluttered the men in unison.

"What a good idea," blethered the Forester. "Why did *I* not think of that?"

"What an excellent suggestion," Jack agreed hastily.

"Well this is *great*." Felicia cried, having recovered from her stunned silence. "Here we are, in imminent danger of being arrested, and all you two can do is gawp at my handmaiden's chest."

Hearing this, Marion turned her back on them. With some struggling beneath the few remaining bandages, she hitched a garment up from round her waist.

"Bloody straps!" she muttered as she slid these over her shoulders.

"Now keep yourself covered up," Felicia snapped. As her maidservant slank back into the shadows, she turned to admonish the men. But once she'd harangued them into a shamefaced silence, she returned to the subject in hand: "Well, what *is* to the east of here then?"

"The counties of Leicester and Warwick," the Forester muttered. "On second thoughts, both of those earls are in league with the Baron."

"So what are we going to do?" Felicia cried, wringing her manicured hands.

"There's a place much nearer than that that's called the Coneygre," Jack volunteered. "The Baron used to breed his coneys there." He snorted. "But they couldn't eat 'em; they kept comin' up covered in soot and stinking of sulphur. They dig out sea-coal there now."

"Who do?" Marion asked, stepping forward into the candlelight. A simple white sark now clung lightly to her body. "The coneys?"

"Don't be daft," Jack laughed, trying to hide his embarrassment. "The *miners*. They've found ironstone there as well. It's a pity they can't smelt it with the coal. [2]"

"I'd forgotten about the Coneygre," the Forester said excitedly. "The Baron needs all the iron he can get for the war effort. The point is: everybody there is having to work flat out and they're always on the lookout for new labourers. They're not fussy about where they come from neither."

---

2 A problem that was solved 300 years later by local nob Dud Dudley. Dud's great-great-nephew Abraham Darby left his birthplace in the Wrosne and set up his revolutionary ironworks in nearby Coalbrookdale.

"An aunt of mine keeps an alehouse near to there," Jack said, expanding on his idea. "We can probably stay with her until the hue and cry dies down."

"Great," cried the Forester, slapping Jack on the back. "And the best thing about this is: they work for *money* and not out of duty to any lord or master."

Felicia spluttered with indignation. "If you think that *I'm* going to perform any manual work you can think again."

"Nay, lass," said the Forester soothingly. "You and Marion can keep out of sight in the alehouse while Jack goes out to work. He can black his face to stop himself being recognised. And when he's earned enough money to buy three horses, you can all escape to freedom, wherever that might happen to be."

Felicia stared pointedly at her maid. "There's nothing to stop *her* going out to work."

"No!" said the Forester quickly. "She'd stick out a mile." He stole another quick glance at her. "A couple of miles in fact."

"So how far away is this... Conny-whatsit?" Felicia demanded as Jack tried to stifle a snigger.

"A couple of miles at the most," the Forester answered. "But there's one big snag."

"What's that?" the others chorused.

Returning to the map, he pointed out a boat-shaped outline in the middle of the wavy green line. "That's the Citadel of the Giants, and it lies across your path."

CHAPTER 18

Jack stared at the sketch of the Citadel on the map, wondering why none of the words beside it began with an 'S'. "We shall just have to skirt around it then," he said.

"No way!" said the Forester firmly. "The southern end can be seen from the Priory bell tower, and see, there's a farmstead up at the north end."

"Then we must head for the Brewood nunnery after all," Felicia muttered, obviously still in a huff.

"It's too late for that now," the Forester announced. "The woodcutters will be astir before you clear the Hampton woods." He sighed. "I shall have to take you through the Citadel. If we leave now, we should get to it before midnight."

"That's decided then," Jack said. "You'll stay with us at the Coneygre of course."

"You are including *me* in your plans for the future?" The Forester glanced across at Felicia and noted her grim expression. "I'd thought of showing you the way. No more than that."

"Why yes," Jack declared. "We're all in this together now. Can you get us there without our being seen?"

"I'm sure I can."

"So what *is* this *Citadel of the Giants*, then?" Felicia demanded, staring challengingly at the Forester.

"It's difficult to describe. You'll just have to wait until we get there." His shoulders slumped. "It's a pity that I can't take Butch, though."

"Why not?" Jack asked, staring fixedly at the maidservant. She was combing her hair – turning her head this way and that against the pull of the comb.

"Never mind why not!" snapped Felicia. "I don't want that mangy dog sniffing round *me*."

"Can't you leave him here?" Jack asked, moving closer to Felicia and trying to cuddle her.

"To starve to death?" the Forester said unhappily.

"Could you leave him with somebody else?" Jack asked.

"There's no time to arrange it."

"You'll just have to put him down then," Felicia muttered.

"It seems that I have no choice." The Forester had dispatched many game animals in his time. One sure thrust of his dagger was all that it took to dim the light from their fear-filled eyes. He'd always consoled himself with the thought that he was only putting the poor beasts out of their misery. Surely he could do the same for Butch. After all, he was getting old now. Well, he was for a dog.

"All right," he said. "I'll do it. But first, we must make ready for the journey." He turned to Jack. "I suppose you got that robe from the monks at the Priory." As Jack fidgeted with discomfort, he smiled reassuringly. "Don't worry. That blotchy grey is even better than black for creeping around in the dark. You'll just have to gird it up to stop it snagging on the brambles. Felicia," he added, turning to face her. "You'll have to get rid of that red dress. It is quite unsuitable."

As the highest-ranking person present, Felicia felt that she had the right to make the important decisions, and that included the colour of her dress. However, her fate seemed increasingly to lie in the hands of this swaggering woodsman and she did not like it. She did not like it at *all*.

"I shall do no such thing," she snorted. "This dress is one of my best, and it's worth a lot of money."

"Well we shan't get far if you're wearing it," the Forester said flatly.

"He's right my love," Jack said. Turning to the Forester, he asked: "But what else is there?"

"There's plenty of suitable clothing on the back shelf. I'll pack that dress in one of the saddlebags if it's *that* important."

While Jack and Felicia met each other's gaze, the Forester peered round in search of the maid. "What about you, Marion?"

Seated again at the far end of the table, she was staring at a candle and mumbling under her breath.

"What are you doing, lass?"

"Nothing," she replied, her eyes still focused on the flickering flame.

"Well, come and help your mistress out of her dress."

As Marion shook her head, her curls swayed gently against her slim white neck. Her lustrous eyes disengaged themselves from the flame and stared up into his, daring him to lower his gaze. He turned quickly away, uncomfortably aware that her shift had slipped again.

"My girl," he whispered, struggling to keep his wayward eyes averted. "The sooner you get yourself decently covered up, the easier it will be for me to concentrate on getting us safely away from here."

"And *you* can keep your eyes to yourself as well," Felicia cried, taking a swipe at the back of Jack's head.

The Forester grabbed a candlestick and carried it self-consciously across to the back wall of the cottage.

"There are smocks and tights here," he announced. "You can take your pick, but I only have 'em in Lincoln Green."

"Green is unlucky!" chorused the women.

"Not if you want to keep your freedom it isn't. And while you are changing, I shall go out and saddle up my horse." He turned to Jack, who was peering out through the spyhole and trying to maintain his concentration. "Keep an eye out for intruders, wiltow? I don't want to be taken by surprise again." With a final exhortation for the women to hurry themselves up, he unbarred the door and stalked out.

A short time later, two wails of despair echoed round the cottage.

"These clothes are rough and hairy," came Felicia's outraged voice.

"These tights are all one-legged," Marion wailed. "There are no gussets in them."

In their separate locations, both men grinned.

*

In a stable at the far end of the yard, a tethered horse pawed impatiently at the ground. The saddle and the bags had been strapped on her, one of the latter containing the scarlet dress. The Forester's sword and crossbow hung down on one side of her neck – a coiled rope on the other.

Outside the door, her owner knelt beside a dog kennel. Butch's head rested warm and comfortingly on his thigh. While his left hand's fingers scratched the hound's brindled scalp, those of his right hand groped for the handle of his dagger. He remembered how he'd used its blade to administer the *coup de grâce* to animals and fallen enemies alike. Now it was Butch's turn. He slid the weapon stealthily from its sheath. Butch looked up at him adoringly, complete and utter trust shining in his eyes. The animal began to tremble. The dagger moved swift and sure.

*

The Forester marched into the cottage and rammed his dagger into the table.

"I shall come with thee only as far as the Coneygre," he announced as the echo of the impact died away. "After that, you are on your own."

Jack turned away from the loophole in surprise. "Aren't you going to stay there with us?"

"Nay lad. After seeing you safe, I shall hurry back here."

"But why?" Jack asked. "N'artow afraid that the Steward's men will kill you?"

"Of course I am," admitted the Forester. "I shall just have to watch my back." He paused. "It wouldn't be so bad if I had a coat of maile."

"You could have lent mine with pleasure," Jack said. "My gran bought it with her crustade money. She said that she couldn't afford to take any chances where my safety was concerned. Whatever the cost."

"She was right about that." The Forester stroked his whiskered chin. "But don't worry about *me*." He noted Felicia's continued hostility. "While I'm at the Coneygre, I shall ask one of the blacksmiths to shape a sheet of iron to cover my back. I saw Longshanks wearing one at Falkirk." He grinned. "I might get a piece to cover my chest an' all."

"But why *aren't* you staying there with us?" Jack asked, doubting if he was man enough to protect the women by himself.

"Butch!" said the Forester simply. "When it came to it, I could-nay kill him."

Before Jack could pass further comment, the Forester marched back to the open door. "We'd better get going," he urged. "The moon is already halfway up to its peak. I want to be back here and acting the innocent when they come looking for you."

As he disappeared out through the doorway, he yelled back over his shoulder.

"ARE YOU WOMEN GOING TO TAKE ALL NIGHT?"

*

The track through the forest would have been scarcely noticeable in broad daylight. Yet even in the darkness of that night, the Forester led the way without hesitation. Slashing at the brambles with his sword, he led his packhorse gently by the reins. Felicia sat uneasily in the saddle, flinching at every rustle in the bushes on either side, but seemingly intent on maintaining a haughty silence. Marion sauntered along at a safe distance behind the horse. She was the most relaxed of them; the candle-spell always ensured her safety in times of danger.

Jack made an anxious rearguard; an arrow on his bowstring and a dozen more rustling in his belt. He could just about see Felicia in the distance. He was sorry that he'd upset her, but he'd only been *looking* at her maidservant. How could any man not? Even the old Forester couldn't take his eyes off her until she'd got herself decently covered up.

There she was now, swaying along just a few feet away in front of him. Although indistinct in the shadows, he still couldn't ignore the power conjured up by her presence – especially with his robe girded up around his waist. Was the Devil trying to tempt him once again? If so, women must be his accomplices. Well, *some* women certainly were.

Tripping over a root, he pulled himself together. As soon as he was able to get Felicia to himself, he'd tell her that he loved her; that he'd loved her since first setting eyes on her, and that no other woman could ever come between them. Then hopefully she'd return his affection once more.

They toiled up through the dark and dripping woodland, 'til the Forester stopped and crept back along the column.

"Jack," he whispered when he'd got within hearing distance, "we're not very far from the outside walls of the Citadel. I know of a secret entrance. If we reach it before midnight, we should be able to get in without the risk of being seen."

"Won't the giants object?" Jack asked half-jokingly. To him, giants existed only in his grandmother's stories.

His mentor stood so stiff and silent that even in the darkness, Jack knew that he was being scowled at.

"No!" said the Forester shortly. "There's no need to fear *them*."

After patting his young companion on the shoulder, he moved back along the line. Passing Marion without speaking, he sidled up alongside Felicia's mount. "Do you think that your father will have discovered your absence by now?"

"Almost certainly not," came the cautious reply. "I had my own room in one of the donjon towers. We crept down the servants' stairs while everyone else was asleep. I'm sure we got out without our being seen."

"All right then," muttered the Forester, sure of nothing. "Onward to the Citadel."

CHAPTER 19

The woodland floor sloped ever more steeply upwards. When the clay became so slippery that it was hard to retain their footing, the Forester halted and uncoiled his length of rope. After belaying one end to the saddle on which Felicia perched, he looped its middle around Marion's slim waist. The other end he tossed to Jack. As they continued to climb, the trees gave way to bushes; then the bushes died away in their turn. Fronted by a scree of mud and rubble, a dark expanse of rock rose up before them. Stretching away on either side, it blocked the way ahead.

"Vwa *Lah*," announced the Forester. "The Citadel of the Giants."

"So *that's* what this place is," Jack said, scrambling up beside him. "I've often wondered, when I've seen it from the castle. Nobody there could tell me much about it. Of course," he added slyly, "we are not allowed in the deer-park without the Baron's permission." He peered up at the unseen heights above. "If you're hoping to use that rope to climb up there, it isn't long enough. Not by a long chalk."

"Nay lad," chuckled the Forester, coiling it up and hanging it from the saddlebow. "This is for our safety later on."

Returning to the shelter of the trees, he set off in the general direction of the Priory. Keeping to the shadows, they skirted the base of the cliff as it curved round towards the east, soon becoming exposed to the glare of the harvest moon. But instead of continuing to swing round to the north, it ran squarely into a cliff of jagged limestone. Initially as tall as the first, this other escarpment decreased in height until hidden among the treetops, a furrow's length nearer to the town.

"Do we have to go round that?" Jack asked. "Surely that will take us too close to the Priory."

"*I* told *you* that," the Forester muttered bluntly. "As you can see: this side of it is still shaded by the moon. It will stay that way until shortly after midnight. That's why I've been trying to get here first."

Hidden in the band of shadow, the fugitives climbed to the confluence of the cliffs. But instead of these coming into contact, a narrowing cleft filled with boulders and rubble ramped up to impenetrable darkness.

"You are *not* thinking of taking us up *there*?" Felicia cried, aghast.

"Yes I am," replied the Forester. "It's the only way in." As he began to remove dead branches from the entrance he added: "I call this 'Desperation Alley', because you need to be pretty desperate to risk going up it."

Felicia peered disdainfully into the chasm.

"Aren't you going to light the lant-horn then?"

"Not just yet," the Forester said as he cast the last branch aside. "If I use my tinderbox out here, the noise will carry for miles. However …" He skidded back down to the horse and unbuckled a saddlebag. "This should deaden the sound." He tugged out the scarlet dress.

"Mind what you're doing with that," Felicia snarled. "I don't want it ruined."

Without another word, the Forester carried the otherwise useless bundle up into the cleft. To the rattling of rolling rubble, his companions heard him striking steel on flint. It took many sharp and noisy blows before he was able to present a glowing scrap of tinder to the candle. But once the flame had caught, he shut the lant-horn's flap and plunged the chasm into darkness once again.

"Pass that to me," Felicia ordered as he returned.

"Not on your life. This is for one purpose only: to help my horse find footholds on the scree."

Felicia pouted, but said nothing more as the Forester led the way up into the fissure.

At first, the going was not too bad; just a rising slope of clay and rubble. A little way up inside, two slabs of rock leaned together like a pair of gossiping women.

"I call these the Praying Hands," the Forester announced as he stood beneath them. "As you can see, there's headroom enough for a man *or* a horse to enter, but not for a woman *on* a horse."

To her great disgust, Felicia had no choice but to dismount. To her even greater disgust, the so-called Forester expected her to carry a saddlebag.

"You can have the lightest one my *laydee*." He handed her the bag that contained her precious dress once more. "It's only fair that *all* of us should share the burden."

"Marion will carry it," Felicia declared, turning her back to insert a slab of limestone into the bag.

"I'll take that one as well," Jack said. "It looks much too heavy for a young wench such as her."

"That you will NOT," Felicia cried, thrusting the loaded saddlebag at her servant. "Marion will do as I say. It is no business of yours."

Jack shrugged, although he couldn't hide his anger at the snub.

With the saddlebags shouldered by Jack and Felicia's servant, all three were linked to the saddlebow with the rope. The Forester led his horse through the Praying Hands – the others then forced to follow him up the fissure. Scrambling up the scree-slopes and holding onto boulders, they felt for the firmest footholds through the thin leather soles of their shoes. Occasionally, one of them slipped, threatening to take them all skidding down the slope. Fortunately, their lifeline to the horse held firm, although even *she* needed help when the rubble gave way beneath her hooves. After much cursing and complaining, they reached the top at last.

The Forester stopped and tugged his friend aside.

"Before we go any further, let's take a look at the castle." Seizing Jack by the hand, he led him out onto the ridge that had screened their approach. On the opposite side of the valley, Dudley Castle squatted menacingly on its hill.

"Can you see any torches burning there?" he asked. "My eyes aren't so good these days."

"Not a single one."

"So Felicia was right about getting away unseen." The Forester spoke with an audible easing of tension. Turning to leave, he noticed the Priory in the vale. The great western wind-eye glowed with coloured light. "They are looking for you down *there* though."

"They might not be. They always light lots of candles there at night."

"What are they like?"

"Who? The monks? I only met a few of 'em. Some of 'em are all right."

The Forester scanned the houses on the distant skyline. Silhouetted against the silvered sky, all appeared dark and peaceful. "Well the good folk of Dudley are all sleeping in their beds."

"The good folk may be," Jack said knowingly, "but just because the curfew has been called, it doesn't mean that there's nobody sneaking about."

Declining to comment on that, the Forester led the way back to the women. From here on in, the canyon opened out onto a dark uneven plain – both sides hemmed with enormous ridges of rock. Their topmost crags gleamed like giants' clotheslines full of washing.

"So this is the Citadel," Jack murmured with wonder. "It looks big enough to hold the whole of Dudley town."

"This is it, lad," confirmed the Forester, spreading out his arms as if to claim it as his own. "Only a race of giants could have built a place as big as—"

"Excuse me for asking," interrupted Felicia, "but if this is supposed to be a Citadel, where are all the houses?"

She had a point. There wasn't a single dwelling to be seen – just huge blocks of greyish rock, dotted about the plain like slumbering sheep.

"I don't know who, or what the giants were afraid of," the Forester said quietly, "but whatever it was must have got in and sacked the place completely. Using fire, most likely."

As Felicia lapsed once more into resentful silence, Jack picked up a piece of loose rubble. When he held it up to the lant-horn beam, the surface showed no signs of burning. He turned the fragment over and held it closer to the light.

"Hey, there's a shell in here like those I've seen at the castle." He held it out for his mentor to see and added: "I've also seen 'em down a well near Dudley town."

"That just goes to show how busy the Devil has been," the Forester said while staring into the distance.

Jack tossed the fragment down, the impact sounding deafening in the silence.

"Hell's teeth!" The Forester gazed anxiously round at the plain. "Don't make so much noise. Who knows who or what might be lurking here."

"Well, it won't be the giants," Jack muttered. "Those cliffs are too well-seated in the ground to have been put here by mortal men – even gigantic men. From what I've seen, these rocks all join up underneath the ground."

"You've got some very strange ideas," the Forester said, gathering in the slack of his horse's reins, "but you'd have a hard time proving that one [3]." He tugged the animal into faltering motion. "Come along my girl," he crooned. "We've still got a long way to go."

With the moon now hidden by the ramparts, the fugitives entered a dark expanse of scrubland. Here and there, pollarded willows raised twiggy hands to the moonlight high above. The boulders now resembled slumbering oxen.

"That's the Giants' Grave over there." The Forester was pointing straight ahead. Beyond their band of shadow, a tree-covered mound rose like a giant molehill in the distance. "You can stop and get your breaths back there."

No one spoke. All were too exhausted and afraid.

After resting awhile on the tree-covered tump, the Forester freed the reins from the branch to which he'd tied them.

"The way out is over there," he declared, staring out at some nondescript spot on the eastern rampart. "Follow me." Once down on the plain, he moved off cautiously – all too aware of his shadow stretching out on his left. His companions followed in line astern, silent and ever fearful of hearing the sounds of pursuit. They hadn't gone far when:

'CRACK!'

---

[3] Proved in the 'Industrial Revolution' when the limestone was mined extensively from underground galleries.

The noise had come from somewhere up ahead. It could have been the snapping of a twig or the sharp percussion of steel on flint. Either way, it meant that they were not alone. The Forester froze, his hand upraised. Crouching low, he gestured for the others to retreat back to the tump. Cautiously they did so, leading the horse into the shelter of the trees. Once tethered there, she stood motionless and quiet; resigned to this after many years of stalking. The Forester dropped to one knee and listened intently. There came a sudden thundering of hooves and something huge and black hurtled towards him in the moonlight. He flung himself down with his crossbow pushed out in front.

CHAPTER 20

Unable to aim high while lying on his stomach, the Forester rolled over onto his left-hand side. Using that forearm as a strut, he raised the crossbow clear of the ground. Although the bolt was in its groove and with the string primed ready to shoot, his fingers were still between the triggering bar and the stock. He hadn't quite got them out when the dark shape was upon him – then above him – and behind him. Having recognised the gleam of tusks as the beast soared over, he listened to the drumroll of its landing. As the sounds of the animal's departure faded away into the night, he chided himself for getting caught unawares. Yet he knew that he'd been lucky; a wild boar could be deadly if it found you on the ground.

Rising unsteadily to his feet, he slipped his fingers back above the triggering rod.

"DAMN YOU, YOU SWINE."

A man's voice. It came from somewhere out in front and over to the right. Once more, the Forester flopped onto the ground and lay stiffly on his belly. Of all the rotten luck. What a time to run into a poacher. And there could be more than one; it would take at least two men to carry a boar as big as that. Normally, he would withdraw quietly and go to summon help. Since that was out of the question, what should he do now? Shout out and try to convince the intruders that they were about to be apprehended? No! The fewer that knew that he was there the better. He should just lie low and wait until they'd departed. They had better look sharp about it. Dawn was fast approaching.

He looked around for a hiding place. Not very far away, a large block of limestone lay shadowed by the moonlight. But to reach it, he would have to cross open land, and therefore be in full view of the interlopers. Still lying on his belly, he inched towards the boulder, slithering from hollow to hollow with the crossbow pushed out in front. Its limb encountered something stiff and unyielding. An arrow protruded at an angle from the earth. He ran his fingers along the fletchings. Aligned with the shaft, here was no spiral twist to steady a broad-headed arrow in flight. He tugged the arrow out and felt the pile. Just as he thought: a bodkin point, forged sharp and slender for penetrating maile. This arrow may have been intended for bringing down the boar, but it hadn't been released by any common poacher. But what would a military man be doing so close to Dudley town? In partial answer to the thought, a second man's voice broke the silence.

"Are you all right, Hugh?" This speaker was over to the left of the first, and he'd sounded much further away. So he was right about there being more than one.

"Yeah!" The first voice replied. "I've missed him again. I'm just going to fetch my arrow."

"Leave it until morning," commanded the second voice. "Get back to your post before Wynterton finds out that you've left it."

There came a grumble, a momentary flash of polished steel, and then all was quiet again.

So the Wyntertons were hiding in the Citadel – the clan behind the slaying of Lord Roger. What were they up to *this* time?

The Forester replaced the arrow just as he'd found it – after first taking note of its angle of arrival, the direction from whence it came and the depth of its penetration into the ground. Using his knowledge of a military bow when used for close work, he judged that the archer was about thirty yards away. That would put him close to the eastern rampart. He'd sounded nearer. It was amazing how sound could travel when close to the ground.

By continuing to slither from one depression to another, he managed to reach the boulder unobserved. Its shadowed side had an overhang into which he now compressed himself, spreading his cloak around to blend in with the rock. He hadn't bargained for *this*.

How many men were out there? It might be just the two. It could be more. A lot more. He must find out. Leaving his helmet behind in the overhang, he inched forward in the shadow of the boulder. He paused. When all remained silent, he left its shelter behind, wriggling with his crossbow out in front.

He seemed to have been crawling for ages when the scrape of steel on steel alerted him to the presence of armed men. Taking cover behind a convenient slab of limestone, he held his breath and listened. When quite sure that hadn't been seen, he raised his head again. Just beyond his hiding place, the ground sloped steeply down to the eastern rampart. The rustling came from within that coal-black hollow, together with the scents of woodsmoke and roasting venison.

He couldn't stay there. He felt too exposed. A little way over to his right, two large boulders lay close together on the rim of the depression. If he could manage to squeeze in between them, he should get a clearer view without putting himself in danger. An inch at a time, he retreated backwards from the hollow. At what he judged to be a safe distance, he slithered sideways until directly behind the gap. Creeping forward again, he squeezed between the rocks.

Lying full-length along the fissure and with his cloak spread out above him, he peered down into the darkness of the hollow. Figures were crouched beside an ember pit. Weapons were being sharpened in the shadows. As he lay straining his eyes to penetrate the gloom, he heard a sudden commotion over to his left. The ground throbbed with the impact of galloping hooves. The air became alive with the chinking of harnesses and maile. Horses whinnied and snorted. Reinforcements were arriving. The situation was getting rapidly worse.

"Who goes there?" The restrained but urgent challenge had come from the suddenly silent depression.

"Be at ease, soldier," came the curt reply. "Walter de Wynterton comes to assume command."

Walter de Wynterton. That was the nob who'd sent Lord Roger's killer.

"Right you are, Sire," replied the unseen guard. "Yessir! All's well, *Sire*. Thirty men present and ready to go, *Sire*."

"Very well, sergeant. Take me to Swynnerton will you? And then get somebody to see to our horses."

"Certainly Sire. Anything else, *Sire*?"

"No. That will be all."

There followed the sounds of tinkling tackle and the plodding of hooves and footfalls.

This was terrible. The way out was blocked and it was too late to try to reach another. With a louder squelching of boots in mud, two figures approached the bottom of the incline … halting just below the Forester's hiding place. With his head completely covered by his cloak, he held his breath and listened.

"Is everything ready for the attack?" Wynterton again, sounding even more imperious than before.

"Yes Sire," replied an underling. "Three wagon-loads of arms are in position by Dudley's Horsepool. We've hidden them under vegetables as instructed."

"They are well guarded, of course?"

"Yes, Sire. By two of our best men disguised as sod-tillers …" The speaker paused, as if unsure whether to continue.

"Get on with it, man. We haven't got all night."

"Sorry, Sire. A detachment is in the Old Park, where the boundary hedge is closest to the Priory. They will enter the town in procession, all wearing black priest's robes. Then on the stroke of noon, they'll begin to relieve the shoppers of their money. (Gasp) And when the guards in the castle sally out to stop this happening, the men that you see here will attack its gate while it's poorly defended."

"Good," said Wynterton with audible relief. "It seems that you have everything in hand … though 'tis a pity that the moon is at its fullest. But at least we can see where we are going in this accursed place. What did you say it was called?"

"Our agent called it the 'Rosnee' or summat like that. He said as it means a link in a chain."

Wynterton guffawed loudly. "Hah! A suitable name for the last link in the chain between our lands and De Somery's hated fortress." He chuckled quietly to himself. "He's away supporting his King at Berwick. Lancaster's up there too, and by the time they have driven out the Scots, we shall all be back home with De Somery's ill-gotten gains in our coffers. You *have* arranged for false heraldry to be left behind, I hope?"

"Yes, Sire. We shall leave one of Lancaster's old war-banners when we go."

"Considering how the Earl has been behaving of late," said Wynterton softly, "no one will believe that he wasn't behind our assault. Very good, sergeant," he added, somewhat louder. "Carry on. Doubtless I shall see you in the castle once it's taken. I assume that our presence here is secret?"

"Yes, Sire. Our spies report no unusual activity in either the castle or the town."

"Very good, sergeant. That will be all."

In spite of the coldness of the ground and of the massive chunks of rock on either side, the Forester's brow had broken out with sweat. Although he'd promised to help Jack and the women to escape, his mates at the castle were in danger. What the hell should he do now?

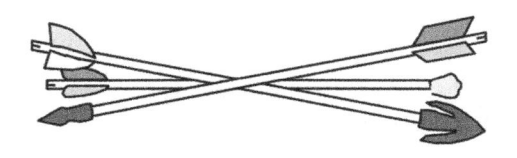

CHAPTER 21

Appalled by what he'd just heard, the Forester shuffled backwards from his hiding place. Hauling his cloak around his shoulders, he made for the distant tump.

"*Keee-veeek!*" An owl screeched in the darkness somewhere behind him. It was answered by another from the direction of the castle.

The Forester froze. Turning slowly around, he scanned the moonlit plain. Nothing moved. Perhaps it was a screech owl, after all. Oh no, it wasn't! Those calls did not ring true. He must have been observed.

*

Back in the encampment, the owl calls had alerted the commander.

"What was that, sergeant?" he demanded.

"Alarm calls, Sire. I shall send out messengers to find out why."

The man departed, returning sometime later.

"Something's happening in the castle, Sire. Torches are being carried along the battlements. They must have got wind of our presence after all."

*

The Forester crouched, motionless and fearful. He could hear a commotion in the encampment and a flash of reflected moonlight showed that at least one soldier had climbed up onto the plain. Keeping a boulder between himself and the enemy, he crept back to the tree-covered tump. "There are soldiers back there," he gasped, "and I think they might have seen me." He scanned the plain for signs of pursuit. So far: there weren't any.

"What shall we do?" Felicia cried, wringing her mud-covered hands in desperation.

"There's not much that we *can* do. They're blocking the only way out on this side of the Citadel."

"It's obvious what we should do," Felicia retorted. "We've got to return to the castle and warn my father of the danger."

"Oh yes!" Jack muttered. "And what d'you think will happen to *us* then?"

"Hell's teeth?" groaned the Forester suddenly.

"What have you seen?" Jack asked, following the direction of his friend's stare. "Are they coming after you?"

"Not yet. But it won't be long before they are. I left my helmet behind near the edge of their hiding place."

"That was very stupid," Felicia taunted. "Do you think they'll have found it?"

"I don't think so. At least, not yet. I left it in the shadow of a boulder." He snorted with self-reproach. "But as the Moon moves round, it'll shine on it. Then it'll light up like a hundred thousand glow-worms. More fool me for keeping it so highly polished. It's only a matter of time before they come looking for its owner."

"How long, would you say?" Jack asked.

"An hour at the most."

"That gives us time to escape back the way that we came," Felicia declared.

"No it doesn't. They're mobilising now, so they'd see us. We are trapped here."

Jack crept to the edge of the mound to get a clearer view out over the plain. "Well I can't see any of 'em moving about. It's all as silent as the grave."

"That's *it*!" cried the Forester, excitedly.

"*What's* it?" Jack asked, turning anxiously round.

"THE GRAVE. This isn't called the Giant's Grave for nothing. I spent most of my childhood up here. As I remember: there used to be a loose slab of rock at the north end of the tump. It was much too heavy for us little lads to lift, but it sounded hollow when we jumped on it. It might provide a good place to hide."

*

In spite of the ancient hawthorn that now hung over it, the Forester soon discovered his childhood slab. It was smaller than he remembered, being not much more than two feet square. The channel that he'd once dug round it had long since filled with earth, so the men set about digging it out again with their knives.

"Try not to scrape the stone," the Forester urged quietly. "The sound might carry and we don't want them to hear us."

"Sorry!"

Soon they had excavated a slot all round the slab, as deep as their blades could reach. Inserting their fingers beneath a convenient edge, they heaved.

"Leeeeeeeft."

The rock refused to budge; it sat so snugly in its ancient bed.

"Agaaaeeeeeen."

This time it *did* move, just a little. As they paused to regain their strength, the Forester turned impatiently to the women.

"Don't stand there gawping. Come and give us a hand."

"You ordered us to keep watch," Felicia reminded him.

"You can do that while you are helping."

"So could *you* if it comes to that!"

In the silence of affronted indignation, all four inserted their hands beneath the slab. They lifted.

"Heeeeeve."

Instead of rising up like a trapdoor would have done, the slab slewed round, held fast by one reluctant corner. A sickening stench welled up from the hole exposed.

"Hell's mouth!" Jack muttered.

"Let us hope that it isn't," said the Forester, lying full-length on the ground. He opened up his lant-horn and lowered it into the cavity. "May Christ protect us," he added as he peered inside.

"What can you see?"

"Give us a chance," came the muffled reply as the Forester withdrew his head. "There's a tunnel of some sort leading off underneath the mound. Bits of the roof have fallen in, but there's room in there for us all." He turned to Felicia. "You go first."

"You don't expect me to go down *there*?"

Jack put his arm around her shoulders. "It's the safest place," he murmured into her ear.

"But it's dirty and horrible and probably full of spiders. Marion, you go first."

"*I'm* not afraid of spiders," the younger woman said. "Or of spirits for that matter. Pass me the lant-horn wiltow?"

Ensuring that her tunic was tucked beneath her loins, Marion swung her legs down into the gaping cavity. After some ooh-ing and ah-ing, the rest of her followed suit. She was gone. Almost immediately, her head reappeared. "It's all right, my lady. There's nothing much down here. Just gravel and dust, and not a single spider."

After taking the same precautions with her tunic, Felicia followed her down into the hole. Soon all four were sitting inside the tomb and leaning back against its massive limestone uprights – Jack and Felicia a little apart from the others. With his arm around her shoulders, he felt her shiver.

"Take heart, my love. At least we are in this together."

She shrugged. "And what a fine place this is that you've got me into."

It *did* smell of dampness and decay. The Forester turned his lant-horn round to shine down the length of the tunnel. They could not see its end.

"Well whoever was buried here," he announced, "must have been more than twenty feet tall. Truly, he was a giant of a man."

"Or woman," Marion added quietly.

"Now *there's* a thought," the Forester murmured, standing and hauling himself up through the hole in the roof.

Felicia leaned over and poked Jack's arm. "I thought you said that there was nothing down here to worry about. So what's *that* in the corner?"

"Where?"

She picked up the lant-horn and directed its beam onto a foot-high heap of rubble.

"What are *those* then? Twigs?"

Several bones protruded from the pile ... and the skull that glared back from the top confirmed that they were human.

"It seems that our giant used to eat people," the Forester said, returning to his place and nodding reassurance. "But what concerns me more is how to get that slab back over our heads."

"But what about *my father*?" Felicia protested. "From what you say, those men are about to attack the castle. He's in great danger."

"I am worried about that myself," confessed the Forester after a pause. "And now that we can hide you women down here, I was thinking of lighting a fire out there on the western rampart. When it's seen by the guards at the castle, it'll alert them to the fact that there's something strange afoot. It should also create a diversion in the camp. We might even be able to sneak out when they go to put it out."

"Do you think that it might work?" Felicia sounded not quite so antagonistic.

"I shall stay to guard the women," Jack declared, squeezing Felicia's arm.

"Oh no you won't," said the Forester sharply. "For one thing, it will take both of us to shift that slab back into place. For another, I shall need your help to build the beacon."

"You will leave the lant-horn behind of course," Felicia said while reaching for their only source of illumination.

"No!" snapped the Forester, whipping it away. "I shall need this for lighting the pyre. Flint and steel would make too much noise."

"*You expect us to sit here in the dark?*" Felicia's wail echoed ghost-like in the confined space.

"Be quiet girl," the Forester scolded. "You'll bring our enemies down upon our heads."

Jack hugged her stiffening shoulders. "If they're within ear-shot, you are more likely to scare 'em off. It won't be for long," he added, trying to sound encouraging. "And you'll have the spare clothes to wrap yourselves up in."

"And what about those bones?"

"Oh *those!*" Jack scrambled over to the pile and tried to pick one out. It crumbled into dust as soon as he touched it. "They must have been here for ages. There's no need to worry about *them*."

"And don't worry about being able to breathe," the Forester said. "When we slide the slab back over you, we'll leave a gap for air to get inside."

"We'd better do as he says," Felicia muttered, her voice more resentful than ever. "He thinks he knows it all."

"In this case, I think that he *does*," Jack said, and planted a kiss on her forehead. "Remember that I love you." He hugged her close before following his friend up and out through the hole.

While there was still enough light to see, Felicia rounded on her servant. "I'll have my dress back now." As Marion discovered the rock inside the saddlebag, her mistress sniggered. "That'll teach you not to flaunt yourself in front of my man. You'll get much worse than *that* if you dare to tempt him again."

Unable to deny the accusation or make any kind of protest, Marion draped the dress round her mistress's shoulders.

So while the women tried to make themselves comfortable in the tomb, the men slewed the slab back over their heads. Clumps of turf were pressed around its edges, with a hollow piece of log for ventilation. They then bestrew the whole area with twigs and leaves.

"That should do it," the Forester announced at last. "Even if the soldiers *do* come up onto the mound, they won't know that anyone's been here, especially in the shadow of this tree."

"What if they've got bloodhounds with 'em?" Jack asked, feeling a shiver of fear.

"Not a chance." The Forester gathered up his horse's reins and prepared to lead her down onto the plain. "Baying hounds would give away their presence just as Butch would have given away ours."

The moon had moved round to the west and dropped lower in the sky, so the shade of the rampart extended almost to the tump. Appalled at having to abandon his beloved Felicia, Jack followed his mentor to the safety of that shadow. On reaching the base of the crag, they set about gathering kindling for the beacon. This proved to be more difficult than expected. There were sticks and twigs in plenty, but most were either too damp to burn, or brittle and liable to crack. Fearful of opening the lant-horn, they worked in almost total darkness, but nowhere near as total as that which enveloped the women in the grave.

"Where's the best place to put the beacon?" Jack whispered when the saddlebag was full.

"Somewhere that those men can't easily get to. I know the very place."

In the safety of the shadows, they struck diagonally up the slope, following a band of rock that was kinder to the feet. While heading in the general direction of the castle, they kept well below the moonlit crest of the rampart. What had looked like giants' washing when seen from a distance, was a row of enormous slabs of limestone – all strewn in great disorder along the crest. The Forester led his horse among them, following an ancient path of tamped-down rubble. At last they reached his chosen spot, where the castle was clearly visible across the vale. With the interlopers' camp now hidden behind the rampart, they set about building the pyre without delay.

"What now?" Jack asked as soon as it was finished.

"Leave me to light the fire. You get back to the women as quickly as you can."

"Who's going to have the horse?"

"You can take her, and my sword as well. But if you're tempted to use that to lever out the slab, be very careful. We might have to fight for our lives."

So Jack led the horse away, while the Forester waited and watched as the moon crept down the sky towards the high road that led to Hampton. When he judged that his friend had had time to reach the tomb, he took the candle from the lant-horn and used it to ignite the kindling. And when he saw that the beacon was blazing strongly, he scrambled over the escarpment and thus, he 'scarpered'.

*

As the Forester had foreseen, the appearance of a glow on the western rampart threw the interlopers' camp into disarray and panic. Horns were blown. Men threw aside their blankets and grabbed for the nearest weapon; and then disputed over who'd got somebody else's. The sergeant could be heard shouting loudly – trying in vain to exert some form of control. For in spite of their military appearance, these men were little more than an untrained rabble.

It was John de Swynnerton who finally imposed some order. After dividing the men into two unequal groups, he dispatched the smaller one to extinguish the fire. The other he formed into a ragged line abreast and sent them fanning out across the plain.

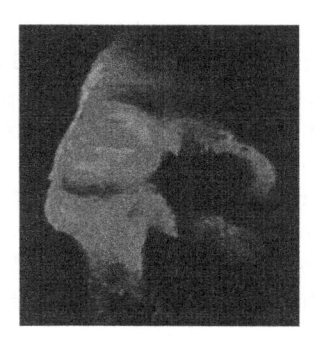

CHAPTER 22

Now back in deep shadow, the Forester picked his way down the inside of the rampart. Although confident that he couldn't be seen from below, the sounds of his descent could carry in the stillness of the night. His beacon would have been seen by the lookouts at the castle. It had certainly been seen by the enemy. Bright pinpricks of light had appeared in the distant encampment. The counterfeit hooting of owls rang out across the plain.

With the surefootedness of one accustomed to prowling about at night, he loped down the band of slightly smoother rock. But before he reached the bottom, the points of light had become a twinkling line. Already it was halfway to the tump. Hopefully Jack had already joined the women. On second thoughts, it might be better if he hadn't. The entrance to the tomb was well hidden when they'd left it, and his friend might be caught while trying to dig it out.

As the Forester stood squinting at the distant torch-line, a stone rattled down in the darkness above and behind him. Something snorted nearby. A large shape loomed up out of the jumbled shadows. A muzzle nuzzled at his elbow.

"Jess! What are you doing here?"

With the horse nibbling affectionately at his sleeve, he heard groaning coming from further up the slope. He recognised the timbre of that voice.

"Jack?" he whispered. "Is that you?"

"Forester? Thank God you've come. I've twisted my ankle." Rubble tumbled in the darkness. "I've been trying to get back on that bloomin' horse of yours, but it won't – ouch – let me."

"Let's get you out of here," the Forester muttered as he helped his young friend up into the saddle. "Wynterton's men'll be here soon."

"But what about the women?" Jack wailed. "I must protect my Felicia."

"Hush. It's too late for that now. Our enemies are already on the tump. See?"

Down on the distant tumulus, torch-flames blinked as they were carried among the tree trunks.

"The women should be safe in there, what with all that stuff we scattered over the entrance. It's *us* that's in the greater danger now."

"Got any ideas about what we should do?"

"Only the one," said the Forester, gathering up the reins. "Desperation Alley."

*

Some time later, the pair had entered the crevasse and were halfway down its succession of rubble-strewn scree-slopes. From one point of view, it was fortunate that the approaching dawn was lighting up the way; Jess could find her footing without the need of the lant-horn. From another, it was disastrous. Having extinguished the beacon fire, the soldiers were clambering quickly along the rampart's crest. Soon they would be above Desperation Alley.

As Jack dismounted to allow Jess to squeeze between two boulders, a cry echoed down the chasm. "There they are! There's only the two of 'em."

An arrow glanced percussively off the rock above Jack's head and skittered off down the scree. Another followed – again without tasting blood.

"Save your arrows," cried a powerful voice above. "You'll never get them while they're under that ruddy overhang."

Stones slid and rubble rattled as the fugitives scuttled further on down the canyon.

"YOU AND YOU: GO DOWN THERE AND GET 'EM. DEAD OR ALIVE, but preferably dead. We don't want witnesses."

135

Although those last words had been less distinct, as though the speaker had turned away, they rebounded back and forth down the length of the chasm. "The rest of you come with me," the voice continued angrily. "Now that we've lost the element of surprise, we shall have to storm the castle by force of arms. Catch us up when you've killed 'em." That last command was intended for the pursuers. Its more immediate effect was to speed the fugitives out through the Praying Hands and down into the dark shelter of the woods.

*

Back in his beloved forest, the Forester led his horse and her crippled rider along paths known only to himself. Not wishing to leave any traces of their passage, their progress had to be agonisingly slow. And since the pursuers had no need for caution, they were rapidly gaining ground.

"It's no good," the Forester admitted finally. "I can't shake 'em off. We shall have to stand and fight. How is that ankle o' yours?"

"A bit easier, thanks," Jack lied, peering round at their immediate surroundings. Above the dark-leafed treetops, the sky was growing brighter. "See that tree?" He pointed further down the slope to where a massive trunk stood black against the gleam of a distant clearing. "Set me down there and carry on going – taking the horse away with you." He snorted with regret. "If I hadn't broken the bow when I fell off her, I could have picked them dastards off like sitting ducks." He shrugged. "But if you leave me your sword, I should still be able to take 'em both on. I've had enough training, for Goode's sake."

As the Forester slid his weapon from its sheath, Jack looked back the way they'd come. "If they *do* gain the upper hand, I'll take a dive so that you can get a clear shot with the crossbow. There'll only be time for the one, so make it count."

"Teaching your grandmother to suck eggs now are we?"

"I've never *seen* her suck eggs," Jack muttered as they reached the edge of the glade.

The Forester was both surprised and pleased by Jack's willingness to take command of the situation. After helping the younger man to dismount behind the tree, he presented him with his tried and trusted sword. Jack laid the blade on the edge of his hand, where it balanced at one hand's-breadth down from the hilt. It also felt good to hold, for the grip was bound with string. Leather would have allowed more ease of movement, but it could become slippery to sweating palms – as Jack's were now.

The Forester stood back, impressed as his friend gripped the weapon in both hands and took a few well-practised swings. And as he turned and led his horse self-consciously away, Jack raised the blade in front of his face and kissed the tempered steel. In spite of all his training, this was his first (and possibly only) real engagement.

"Yay-sous, Woden or Thunor, please help me now," he whispered above the tumult in his mind. "Thank you," he added as the pain in his foot ceased abruptly. A calm resolve flowed over him, stilling his trembling limbs.

Leaning with his left elbow against the tree, he waited in silence for his would-be killers. But not for long. With the Forester and his horse still visible across the glade, he heard stealthy footsteps approaching through the undergrowth.

"THERE THEY ARE!"

After that one exultant shout, the shadowed woods fell silent once again. Jack strained his ears for the slightest sound. They picked up the faint rustle of flight feathers. An arrow had been withdrawn – either from an archer's belt or from a quiver. Then came a slow intake of breath … the silent pause as a bow string was drawn back. Out from behind the tree trunk protruded the bodkin head of an arrow. Aimed at the retreating Forester, it gleamed wickedly in the dismal light.

Jack hauled back his blade and stepped out from behind his tree. Time slowed almost to a standstill. With all the pent-up power of his back and arms, Jack swung his blade forward in a murderous shining arc. As a consequence of the weapon's fast rotation, its centre of weight moved further down the blade. Jack steered that forceful point towards the bow, striking it just above the archer's grip.

THWACK. The blade sliced into the sapwood of the yew, severing its tawny fibres.

SNAP. Instead of speeding the arrow towards its victim, the tensioned bowstring split the weapon in twain. Splinters flew from the shattered end-grain.

The archer reeled back as Jack's sword sped towards his throat. Unwilling to inflict a mortal blow on a fellow conscript, Jack steered his blade towards his opponent's helmet. That beaten steel was beaten once more as its wearer sagged heavily to the ground. Jack's sword rebounded, quivering like a living thing in his hands. He glimpsed the glint of polished steel above him as another blade sliced down towards his shoulder. The second killer had entered into the fray. With an instinct instilled by many months of training, Jack raised his left elbow and swung his sword up to parry the blow. Hardened steel clashed on hardened steel. Saint Andrew's Cross flashed briefly against a backdrop of dark foliage. Jack stumbled back on his weakened ankle, striving to block the downward slash. But its force was too great and it had struck Jack's blade too close to the tip. Smashing on down, it almost wrenched the handle from Jack's grip. However, its plunge had been diverted. Skidding down and off Jack's sword, it sliced savagely into his side. Pain exploded as the killer cried out in triumph. But too soon. The impetus of the blow swept his blade further on and down, embedding it in the tree. The killer's jubilant expression turned to one of horror. As he struggled to release his weapon from the heartwood, his face came level with the pommel of Jack's sword. But Jack was now off-balance – with his wrists crossed over and touching. With the unthinking skill acquired from repetition, Jack shifted his hold on the handgrip – reversing first the left hand then the right. Insensitive now to pain, he concentrated all his strength on his upper body. With the centre of weight of his weapon now directly behind the pommel, he rammed this with all his might into his opponent's face. Blood anointed the shiny brass ball with crimson as the would-be killer fell across his partner's body.

"The job is done!" Jack's cry of victory rang through the brightening woods.

Now that the danger was past, his pain returned with a vengeance. He slumped groaning to his knees and fell sideways onto the ground. Ignoring him for the moment, the Forester tied their opponents' hands with severed lengths of the bow-string. But as he roped their torsos to the tree, Jack pulled himself together.

"What are we going to do now?" he wailed while writhing about in pain.

"Well we've warned them at the castle of their danger. It's for *them* to deal with now."

"You reckon?" Jack protested weakly. "There's only a few of 'em left there to guard both the castle *and* the town."

"How many would you say?" The Forester had to ask it, in spite of his comrade's plight.

"A dozen at the most. Plus a few blacksmiths and other tradesmen. Do you know how many enemies they'll have to face?"

The Forester thought back. Somebody had said that there were thirty armed men in the Citadel. Then more had arrived to join them. How many flaming torches had he seen fanning out across the plain?

"At least fifty," he said, "plus the two who'm already in the town. And who knows how many are hiding in the park."

"It's not looking good, then," Jack stated unnecessarily.

"Definitely not," agreed the Forester. "Especially if our men sally out to see what's happening in the Citadel."

"Will they fight?"

"Not if they've got any sense," said the Forester bitterly. "Their best course of action is to surrender."

"Then the castle will be plundered," Jack cried. "What will happen when the Baron gets back?"

"I shudder to think."

"Hang on!" Jack said, struggling to sit up. "I think I know where we might get help."

"Before we do anything at all," said the Forester calmly, "let's take a look at that wound of yours." As he lifted the flap of blood-soaked cloth, his friend groaned and fell unconscious into his arms. While trying to staunch the flow with a wad of nettles wrapped up in a diaper, he whistled for his horse to come back up and join him.

CHAPTER 23

Later that morning, Jack was back in Dudley and peering down the well. His wound had been cleaned out, treated with herbs and bandaged. Although the pain was still giving him gyp, he leaned out over the parapet.

"Halloo there," he bawled down into the shaft.

"*Theeeeere…*" answered the well.

"Is there anybody there?" he repeated.

"*Theeeeer…*" echoed the well.

"And WHAT do you think you are doing?"

Startled, Jack looked up into the eyes of a stranger. Well, he assumed that it was a stranger. The upper half of his face was shadowed by a hood, the lower half hidden by the liripipe covering his chin.

"Ah'm." Jack cleared his throat while thinking fast. "I've just chucked in a penny and I'm about to make a wish."

"And what sort of wish would that be, young sir?"

Jack lowered his voice. "Actually, it's a wish for some archers to repulse an attack on the castle."

"And why should bowmen be needed to defend the castle?" In spite of the stranger's apparent scepticism, his eyes betrayed a keen interest.

"Why?" Jack whispered. "Because it would be to their own benefit. Has not the Steward agreed to supply them with grain to feed their families through the famine?"

"Arrr," agreed the man, "but only after we forced him to."

"If the castle *is* captured," Jack retorted, "you can forget about your grain. It'll be carted away by Wynterton's men."

"And what do yer mean by that?"

Jack told him.

"Lord help us," gasped the liripipe-man, anxiety in his eyes. He unhooked a ladle from the wellhead and rattled it around in the bucket that hung above the shaft.

"What's up now?" sighed a voice from the depths.

"That bloke what took our petition is back."

"Whaaaaaa?" The voice from below was louder now, but it still had a hollow ring.

"He says there's trouble brewing. Hang on. I'll send 'im down and he can tell yer 'is self."

In spite of his pain, Jack allowed himself to be sat on the parapet and swivelled around until his feet were in the bucket. To the creak and rattle of the windlass, he disappeared into the depths. A faint splash echoed up the shaft.

"ELLO, ELLO, ELLO! WHAT'S ALL THIS THEN?" Distinctive in his golden tunic of office, the Bailiff was shouldering his way through the gathering crowd. "Break it up now. You know that groups of more'n four are not allowed."

The human screen moved grudgingly aside.

"Will Hawkes!" the official exclaimed. "Fancy seeing *you* here. I hear there's been some trouble in your neck o' the woods."

"Not just trouble," the Forester spluttered. "Wynterton's men are hiding in the Citadel. They're about to attack the castle."

The Bailiff flushed with surprise and anger. "Does the Steward know about this?"

"I'm on my way to tell him."

"I should look sharp about it then," urged the Bailiff, waving him away. As he watched the Old Park Forester mount his mare and turn her towards the castle, he stroked his bristly chin. "Now why should you come down *here* when it's so far out of your way?"

He peered down into the well-shaft. Was that *talking* that he could hear? No! It was only the echoes of the murmuring all around him. Ignoring the peasants who were queuing up with their buckets, he turned away, disquieted. His ears had been playing up of late, and it could be the first sign of some horrible disease. Or perhaps a witch's curse?

When he'd hurried away in search of the local wise-woman, the well disgorged a procession of grim-looking men. Each held a bow and had a quiver full of arrows on his back. Jack emerged last, to be helped up into a hurriedly drawn-up wagon. Ignoring the anxious bystanders, he arranged the archers into pairs and led them purposefully off towards the castle.

*

Fortunately, Jack's knaves reached the castle gate before the attacking force arrived. After erecting a protective line of wicker fencing, they crouched behind it and waited.

For watchers from the town, all that could be seen were the upper limbs of bows. All were tilted back, with their arrows aiming high – in readiness for the soldiers who were marching up from the Priory with the sunlight glittering brightly on their helmets.

Observing what he judged to be a mere rabble barring his way, Walter de Wynterton rode to the head of his column.

"I DEMAND THAT YOU SURRENDER," he bellowed from the saddle of his jet-black warhorse.

"In whose name?" demanded a sentry from the outer gatehouse battlements.

"In the name of Thomas of Lancaster."

"Sod off," came the curt reply.

"Surrender now, or you are all dead men," cried De Wynterton.

An answering shoal of arrows soared above the rustic shield-wall. Arcing across the forecourt, the missiles swooped down on the attackers – nailing maile, piercing plate and skewering unprotected flesh. With screams and curses, the soldiers broke ranks and ran, spurred on by a second volley of speeding shafts. Ignoring the frantic admonishments of their leaders, the men fled back down the road in fear of their lives.

The danger had passed.

*

Several days later, the Steward called for silence as John de Somery, the umpteenth Baron of Dudley, took his seat in the donjon's great hall. His once-golden surcoat was grey with the dust of travel and blotched with rust stains from the maile of his damaged hauberk. Above his head, the faded and tattered banners of past battles stirred slowly in the draught. A newer one on its staff stood propped up between the pair of lancet wind-eyes. Through these came the sounds of hounds baying, of carts being unloaded, of horses being attended to, and of gossip being gossiped.

While the Baron sat silently at his table, his retainers stood around in anxious attendance. Beside the doorway leading out onto the spiral staircase, the Steward was conferring with his henchmen. All three were staring at Jack with hostile intent. He and the Forester stood nervously at one end of the table – Felicia and her maid more decorously at the other. In front of the curtain that screened off the servants' staircase, those worthies cocked their ears for what was coming. Jack's grandmother crouched behind it, quaking in her shoes.

The Baron raised his hand to demand attention.

"First," he bawled, his powerful voice tinged with sadness and regret, "I must inform you about the Scottish Wars." His audience shuffled their feet but otherwise remained silent. "As you've probably heard," he continued, "the siege of Berwick had to be called off when Lancaster abandoned the field. We'd been hoping that, with the Earl and the King united against the Scots, their familial hostility would be healed at last. Together, they might have ruled our country with greater wisdom." He sighed. "But this was not to be. A rumour was circulating that King Edward had ordered the Earl to be killed once Berwick had been retaken."

Jack and the Forester stared at one another. It was only too clear that once you'd upset your superiors, they'd get rid of you when it suited them – no matter how high up you were in the pecking order.

"And while I've been away," the Baron continued angrily, "my enemies have seized their chance to attack my stronghold. Aye, and to falsely implicate Lancaster in the deed. Fortunately, their plans were thwarted." He swivelled around in his throne to stare across at his Steward. "Come over here, willtow? I've done enough shouting at

Berwick."

His official lumbered over, appearing to grow even larger as he approached the table. Nevertheless, he looked distinctly anxious.

"My lord?" he said, his voice abnormally subdued.

The Baron grinned at him with humourless eyes. "I left you to deal with the troublesome peasants."

"Yes, my lord." His Steward nodded nervously in agreement.

"However," his master continued, "their insurrection was stopped by your offer to send out grain."

The Steward looked even more nervous.

The Baron leaned forward and stared up into his eyes. "Did you think that I'd view your actions with disfavour?" He shook his head. "No, my ever-trusted Steward." There was that mirthless grin again. "Nobles all over the country are conducting similar acts of mercy. It's called *'Noh-bless Oh-bleezh'*." He leaned back in his throne. "It seems that I have much to thank you for."

"*That's just not true,*" Felicia cried, bursting with indignation. "He would never have thought of it if my Jack hadn't handed him their petition."

The Steward glared at his daughter. "Silence, girl. You must *never* speak like that to your lord and master."

Ignoring her *lord and master*, she stared defiantly back at him; hands on hips, her scarlet gown glistening in the torchlight.

"*Without my Jack,*" she shrieked, "the Baron wouldn't have much of a stronghold to come back to.*"*

"My daughter lies," her father protested loudly.

"Don't they all?" murmured someone at his rear.

After scowling at his smirking audience, the Steward turned back to the Baron.

"My Lord. Not only was it *me* who stopped the peasants from revolting; it was *me* who enlisted them to repel the attack on this castle." (The peasants, having been excluded from the donjon, therefore had no say.)

"It's my father who is lying," Felicia screamed, projecting malice through her pointing finger. "My Jack did that as well." She gazed across at her beloved and recoiled from his reproving stare. "Well, him and that oaf he calls The Forester," she added grudgingly.

John De Somery slumped back in his throne, dark furrows creasing his forehead. At length, he hauled himself wearily to his feet.

"A word with you in private, Master Hawkes," he said, nodding towards the door to a corner drum-tower.

When the Forester moved away from the table, Jack fell heavily against its edge. His friend had been supporting him all along.

"For Goodes' sake, get him a stool," the Baron shouted.

While a servant hurried to do so, he led the Forester over to the door. And as it banged shut behind them, the onlookers heard the Forester pleading his case.

After what seemed an age of waiting in draughty silence, the door flew open and the Baron and his forester emerged. As they returned to the table, the Baron waved Will Hawkes over to join his seated friend. Then, easing himself into his throne, he glared around like an eagle intent on murder.

"SCRIVENER. PREPARE TO TAKE THIS DOWN."

At his desk beside the nearest lancet wind-eye, the monk from the Priory jerked upright in his chair. Leaning forward to grab his quill, he jabbed it self-importantly into an inkwell.

"Steward!" the Baron said quietly – but loud enough for everyone to hear. "You appear to have coped quite well while I've been away. NOW WRITE THIS DOWN. I therefore make you the manager of our dealings with the peasants."

While the Steward tried in vain to retain his composure, his daughter bristled with exasperation.

"It's my Jack that you should be rewarding, not my father."

The Baron stared hard at Jack, who quailed beneath his scrutiny. "I hear that you've been pilfering our food," he said abruptly.

Jack couldn't deny it.

"However," the Baron continued, "in view of what my Forester has just told me, I shall grant you a pardon for all your misdemeanours." As Jack opened his mouth to stammer out his thanks, the Baron waved him to silence. "I am also prepared to receive you back into my household, although your usefulness as a fighting man could be over."

Although elated by the pardon, Jack had no desire to return to

145

work as a cookney.

"I also understand..." the Baron went on in a slightly less bitter tone of voice, "that you seem to have acquired some talent for diplomacy. Canstow read?"

"Only a little," Jack confessed shamefacedly.

"STEWARD?" It was that officer's turn to jump to his master's voice.

"Yes, Sire?"

"See to it that he learns his letters properly. I expect him to have his diploma within the year."

"Yes, Sire," muttered the official with a noticeable lack of enthusiasm.

"And then," the Baron added with a wicked chuckle, "he can be your assistant."

"So can Jack and I be married then?" Felicia cried with the impetuosity of youth. As she ran around the table to Jack's side, her father thumped down on it with his fist.

"Forgive me Sire, but NAY. I have arranged an excellent match for her and *he* is but a penniless upstart. And as you can see: *he* can't even stand up straight without support."

Jack blushed. He couldn't deny it. What would be the point? Everybody there knew this to be the sooth.

Felicia exploded with fury. "He got that wound protecting this castle from Wynterton's men!"

Jack hauled himself painfully to his feet. "I could never have done it without your forester's help."

"Will Hawkes?" the Baron turned to his woodsman again. "Since I also find myself in *your* debt, I am prepared to overlook the fact that you were helping a fugitive to escape from justice."

"It's just as well that he was," Jack muttered, thinking that none would hear him.

"INSOLENT KNAVE!" roared the Baron, turning to glare at him.

"But my lord," Jack protested. "If we hadn't been in the Citadel, we'd never have found out what Wynterton was planning, *and* we'd never have driven him off."

Sighing deeply, the Baron leaned back in his throne and closed his eyes. In the silent hall, his servants waited breathlessly.

"SO," the Baron cried suddenly, causing everybody else to jump.

"Will Hawkes. In view of what I have learned, I declare that you too are pardoned for your wrongdoings."

As his Forester relaxed visibly, his master continued: "And that includes your laxity in not preventing my brother's murder. Consider yourself absolved of that as well."

With the Forester now looking even more disconcerted by his master's mirthless smile, the Baron continued: "I also decree that the monks shall resume their praying for your immortal soul. GOT THAT DOWN, SCRIVENER?"

The monk jerked violently again. So much so that a droplet of ink dripped from his quill. He stared down at his parchment in horror.

After a warning glance at his Steward, the Baron turned to the loving couple: "Oh, get married if you *must*. It might calm the two of you down." Ignoring the fact that his Steward was having some sort of fit, he nodded at the lancet wind-eyes. "You can live down there with my other quill-pushers. *DON'T WRITE THAT DOWN,*" he shouted hastily. "And you can retain that pretty young wench as your maidservant. Well, you can while we're holding her hostage to ensure that the Welsh stick to their pledges."

Jack smirked. He'd been wondering about her enchanting way of speaking. It also explained the way she'd been behaving.

"Thank you, Sire," he said, embracing his beloved. And as Felicia smiled back up at him, she radiated a beauty that was all her own.

Marion had remained silent throughout – her eyes downcast demurely. She would not be such a fool as to entice her mistress's consort again … heart-stoppingly handsome and brawny though he was. After all, there'd be other young men to help her to pass the time. And if the worst came to the worst, there was always the candle magic.

Behind the servants' curtain, Jack's grandmother wiped away a tear.

"The lucky little bleeder!" she muttered (thankfully).

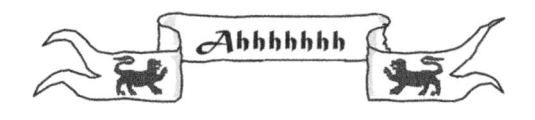

𝔄hhhhhhh

The Author

Having retired from work as an engineer, I suddenly had the time to pursue other interests. But what? Several years earlier, I'd completed an extensive piece of research whose thesis gained me an M.Phil. degree at Birmingham University. Could I write anything with people in it? A short course on creative writing convinced me that I could. But what about? One of the exercises required the portrayal of a building in Dudley. I chose the castle, having long been fascinated by Medieval England. I suppose that this was inspired by Errol Flynn's portrayal of Robin Hood (who is now believed to have been operating at the time of this story). What was I waiting for? Inspiration? It was all around me. To augment my new research, I joined a group of re-enactors who recreate aspects of life in earlier times. With them, I have been able to:

- Amuse visitors to the castle and the zoological gardens that surround it,
- Shoot arrows from the battlements of the Donjon,
- Wield a sword with reasonable safety,
- Prove that wearing maile is no great hardship
- Set my tinder box on fire with flint and steel
- And deafen everybody with my Spanish bagpipes.

The result is this recreation of life in medieval Dudley.
I hope that you enjoy reading it as much as I've enjoyed writing it.